Joan + Doug
Inner peace
happy endings
Lynn

5-10-2007

Don't...
Bless Me Father

by

Lynne Kathleen Pettinger

author**HOUSE**™

1663 LIBERTY DRIVE, SUITE 200
BLOOMINGTON, INDIANA 47403
(800) 839-8640
WWW.AUTHORHOUSE.COM

© 2005 Lynne Kathleen Pettinger. All Rights Reserved.

First published by AuthorHouse 06/07/05

ISBN: 1-4208-3459-2 (sc)

Library of Congress Control Number: 2005902134

Printed in the United States of America
Bloomington, Indiana

This book is printed on acid-free paper.

For:

My Sister
Laraine

My Brother
Lorne

and

My Teacher
Bob Cawley

CHAPTER 1

Annie trembled. Sister Mary Margaret walked toward her holding the hardwood ruler. Her heart was pounding like a rock against her six year old chest as she stared down at the nun's long, skinny feet laced tightly in shiny, black oxfords. "Hold out your hands", she demanded. Annie didn't move. The nun shook Annie's tiny shoulders and again demanded she hold out her hands. Annie held her small, shaking hands before the angry nun. "Take off the mittens", she yelled. She pulled off the red and green stripped mittens that her mother had knit and placed them on the nun's desk. Two hard slams to each hand was her punishment for dropping two peels from her orange in the school yard. "Go home", she said. Annie slipped her mittens on feeling the welts starting to rise on her palms and the sharp tingling in her fingers.

She left the heat of the school and started the long walk home. The wind was blowing hard, snow was piling up and it was getting dark. A half hour later she reached her home. Kicking the snow off her winter boots she stepped into the cozy kitchen. Her mother was setting the table for dinner. "How was your day?" she asked. Annie said nothing, just held out her red hands. "Who did this to you?", her mother asked gently as she held Annie's little hands in her own. The warmth of her mother's hands made Annie feel safe. "Was it Sister Mary Margaret". The tears Annie had been holding back came tumbling down. "Don't worry my little Annie", she said. I'll take care of this tomorrow."

We waited until six o'clock for Dad to get home. Six o'clock was always dinner time. He arrived, said nothing, changed from his work clothes into casual slacks, sports shirt and loafers. He was a good looking man. Annie was always so proud to walk beside him when they entered the Cathedral for Sunday mass. She knew what the ladies were whispering. He was tall, dark and handsome; perfect teeth with a charming smile. Annie could hardly wait for her First Communion ceremony so she could kneel beside him and receive Jesus at the communion rail.

As the family took their places at the dinner table Annie's eight year old brother, Timothy, sitting next to her, fell off his chair. No one laughed. No one spoke. Annie reached over and helped him. He had been doing this for the past several weeks. He was also stumbling and falling when he walked. They gathered hands, said grace and ate with no conversation until Timothy asked Annie why her hands were so red. Mother explained. Father said, "I deserved it, it didn't matter that it was an accident, I should be more careful". At seven o'clock sharp the family rosary was said. Tonight was Annie's turn to lead. When the rosary was said we gathered round the TV and watched Bishop Fulton Sheen tell us how bad we were and we should pray for forgiveness. Father then left and wouldn't return until eleven o'clock. It was a ritual. Where did he go? What did he do?

"Wake up, Annie, time to get ready for school, it's snowing so you will have to leave a bit earlier so you won't be late". Annie crawled from under the warm blanket and stood over the heat vent in the hall while she dressed. She could hear Timothy and her older sister Kate already at the breakfast table. Soon she was out in the cold facing the long walk to school.

Sister Mary Margaret was waiting at the door twisting her long prayer beads, beads with a large crucifix that almost touched the floor. Annie passed by, took her seat and wondered what the day would bring. Nothing like yesterday she hoped. The day passed slowly. It was almost time to go home when Sister Catherine Marie, the Principal, called Sister Mary Margaret to the office. The school bell rang but no one dared move until she returned or severe punishment would be enforced. The classroom door opened and Annie saw her mother. "Come along, Annie", she said. Annie quickly put on her winter coat and boots and reached out for her mother's hand. As they walked from the school Annie knew there would be no more trouble from Sister Mary Margaret. She didn't have to ask, she just knew. Hand in hand, kicking the freshly fallen snow, Annie was happy. She stopped in mid-step, looked up at her beautiful, smiling mother and said, "I love you Mom". Annie loved her mother's face. She was beautiful. Very petite with shoulder length auburn hair, worn in a page boy cut. Dad said she had the Irish temper, but Annie never saw it. She was always quiet, didn't say much but when she spoke, everybody listened.

Her mother reached down and with a red leather gloved hand touched Annie's face. The magic of that touch always gave Annie a feeling of being loved.

CHAPTER 2

The nightly dinner was interrupted by the ringing of the phone. Mom quickly reached for it but said very little. There was no rosary that night, we were just sent to bed. Dad left as usual. Annie wondered again "Where did he go? What did he do?'. To ask would never enter her mind. "Children should be seen and not heard", was a quick reply to any question that was none of her business.

Annie listened quietly as she laid in bed. Mom dialed a number. Seconds passed. She was sobbing into the phone. "I don't know what to do. How could such a thing happen". He was such a healthy, lively baby and now the doctors say it won't be long before he will be in a wheelchair for the rest of his life. There is a special hospital in Montreal. I'm going to take him there. Prayers, novenas, lighting candles won't help. How could God do such a thing to my son?" She hung up. Years passed before she stepped inside a church again.

There was a lot of whispering over the next few weeks and before Annie knew it Mom and Timothy were Montreal bound. She remembered waving as the train slowly gathered up speed and left the station. They would be gone for a week. Kate was in charge. Nightly dinner was never the same. Dad came home, checked on us and then left again. Father O'Reilly dropped in a couple of times that week to make sure we were saying the nightly rosary. We never did.

It was the longest week of Annie's life but finally Mom and Timothy came home. He was wearing a heavy brace on his back. It was suppose to help him but it didn't. He kept falling and soon the wheelchair made its appearance. "This will be fun, Timothy", Annie said. "I'll push you all over the neighborhood and I can jump on the back when we go down a hill. It won't be so bad". But it wasn't fun. Weeks, months went by and Timothy kept falling out of the chair so a special tray and harness was rigged up to hold him in. No more pushing around the neighborhood, no more racing down the hills. A horrible silence fell on the house. Dad was never home.

Father O'Reilly and another priest, Father O'Sullivan appeared at the door one rainy evening. They must have been expected because Dad was home. Tea was served and pleasantries exchanged. The children were sent to their rooms. But Annie sat at the top of the stairs, where she couldn't be seen and listened.

"We haven't seen you at Mass, Rose", Father O'Reilly began. "It is your duty to attend Mass with your children and husband. If you need assistance with Timothy, we can help. He hasn't received his First Communion yet nor has Annie. The next ceremony is scheduled for the first of May. You cannot deny your children this very important step. The rehearsal will be two weeks from Sunday. We expect you there".

"My children will attend, but I will not attend". Her voice was low and cold.

Annie couldn't sleep that night. She kept thinking about the white dress and veil she would be wearing at her First Communion. She would be in the procession with Timothy. How she loved him. It didn't matter that he was in a wheel chair. He was still Timothy, her older brother. She would rush home after school and tell him about her day. She did her homework with him. Although Sister Theresa came twice a week to school him, he was falling behind. Mom spent most of her day looking after him. It was constant care. He could still feed himself but he had trouble with little things, like holding a pencil or even brushing his teeth. Mom did everything and always with a smile. He was never out of her sight.

Two weeks dragged by for Annie but here they were at the Cathedral for the First Communion rehearsal. Father O'Reilly greeted them. There would be forty children partaking of this religious event, twenty girls and twenty boys. The girls were to line up on the left side of the aisle and the boys on the right. Slowly they were to proceed to the altar. Annie took her place and looked around for Timothy. He should have been right across from her but he was at the back of the line. She stepped from her place and walked slowly to the back. Dad was talking to Father O'Reilly. Father O'Sullivan was also there. Annie stood beside Timothy's wheelchair and asked, "Why isn't Timothy in the line across from me? That's how it's suppose to be, that's what we planned?"

"Now, now Annie, this isn't for you to decide. We have decided that Timothy will be brought to the altar before the procession starts. That way the line will be perfect", said Father O'Reilly.

"Well, then I'll be at the altar too".

"No, you will take your place in line".

"No. I won't do it. Not without Timothy".

She ran from the church to her mother who was waiting outside. The priests and her father followed.

"Why are they doing this Mom, why can't Timothy go down the aisle across from me? It isn't fair".

"Sometimes life isn't fair, Annie. Now you apologize to Father O'Reilly and go back and take your place".

With lowered head Annie did as she was told.

CHAPTER 3

The days and months rolled into years. Annie was now ten years old. Sister Theresa didn't come to the house anymore. Mom said she could teach Timothy and do a better job. Sister Theresa wasn't very patient. Annie thought she always smelt sweet. It couldn't have been perfume. Nuns didn't wear perfume. Dad was home earlier now helping with Timothy. He didn't do much just carried him from room to room. He never said very much until one Spring afternoon.

School got out early because of a teacher's meeting. As Annie walked toward the street she saw her father's car parked nearby. Looking around she spotted him getting into the car. She hollered for her father and he turned with a very surprised look on his face.

"What are you doing here, Dad, is everything okay? Is Timothy alright?"

"Yes, everything is fine. C'mon I'll give you a ride home".

This was the first time Annie could remember ever being alone with her father. It was an odd feeling. When the silence became unbearable she blurted out,

"Where do you go after dinner, Dad?".

"Well, young lady, that is really none of your business but I will tell you. I own several race horses. They need a lot of care and each night I go to the stables to feed and water them. They also need to be walked. Now, does that answer your question?".

"Horses! Horses!". Annie couldn't have been more surprised.

"Does Mom know? How long you have had them? Are they girls or boys and what are their names? Do you really race them? I want to go see them".

Of his three children he was fondest of Annie. He watched her grow and enjoyed her enthusiasm. She wasn't a pretty child. Born with an eye defect, her right eye was crossed. Her platinum blonde, long curls were her best feature. She was a mere speck of a thing, very thin. She loved to dance and when asked, "what do you want to be when you grow up?", the answer was always "a dancer". Her mother had her in ballet and tap classes. He thought it was just a stage she was going through. A teacher. Yes, a teacher would be a good job for Annie. His attention went back to his youngest daughter.

"Slow down, Annie, slow down. Sister Theresa told me that your best subject in school was reading but your math is not good. When you get an A in math then I will take you to see my horses. If you're good Sister Theresa may give you some extra help after school".

The next day Annie asked for the extra help and she got it. Three days a week Annie stayed after school and soon caught up. She believed that an A wasn't far away. Mom didn't say too much, she was busy with Timothy but she was also doing a lot of reading about corrective eye surgery. Before Annie knew it she was in Dr. White's office for an eye exam.

"Well, Rose", he said "I think this new surgery can help Annie. Now you must remember this is all new and there are no guarantees but I believe it will work. Now, Dr. Harrison will do the surgery and I'll assist".

Annie sat quietly. "Does this mean that my eye will be like everybody else's? I won't be called those awful names?", she thought. "Oh, God please, let Mom say okay".

"Do you want to think about it, Rose, talk it over with your husband?"

"No, that is not necessary. I want to go ahead with this operation".

On the way home everything was explained to Annie.

"Do you think Dad will say it's okay?", asked the excited child.

"It doesn't matter what he says", thought Rose.

"Annie, you will have this operation and you will have the most beautiful blue eyes anyone could ask for".

Later that night when her husband came home Rose told him about the impending surgery. He didn't agree. He felt it was too risky. What did it matter, her vision was okay. Well, what did it matter what he thought. Rose would do exactly what she wanted as she always did.

Three weeks later Annie had the surgery. It was her first time away from home and she cried so hard the doctors told Rose that the eye wasn't healing and she would be better off at home. A patch had to be worn over the eye for two weeks, drops put in every four hours. Between Annie and Timothy, Rose was a very busy mother but at seven o'clock each night Rose spent "the rosary hour" reading to her young children. It was summer vacation and Kate was a big help. She would put the drops in Annie's eyes and tell her everything was going to be okay. How beautiful Annie was going to be. Kate was always taking care of people. If voices were raised even a little in the house Kate was right there to quiet things down. Sibling fighting never happened. "You mind your own p's and q's", she would say and the arguments stopped there.

The patch and bandages came off Annie's eye. Success. Everyone was very excited especially Annie. Her eyes were straight - they matched. The following day Rose gathered her three children and told them they would be having another brother or sister around Christmas time. On Christmas Day a boy was born, little Joseph. Annie fell in love with Joey. She was now eleven years old and big enough to help. She fed him, rocked him and at the slightest squirm she was at the crib picking him up. If she could just get that A in math life would be perfect.

Sister Theresa was still giving her extra help and she was improving. One particular day after school, Annie was in the cloak room getting her extra math work . She heard Sister Theresa and Sister Mary Margaret enter the room. They were talking.

"The last thing in the world that family needed was another baby. John should have been more careful. What if that child is another Timothy. Rose spends all her time with the children and John is certainly neglected. He works so hard. I thank God that he has his horses. At least he has an outlet from her and those children", sighed Sister Theresa. "I have to leave now and so should you. You've waited long enough. Do you think she will ever grasp math? It is such a struggle for her".

They both left.

Annie couldn't move. She sat in the cloak room bewildered. Ten minutes later she left the school and walked home.

"What did she mean about Joey being like Timothy? And why did she call Dad by his first name, it was always Mr. Thompson when Annie was around and she would get the grasp of math, she really wanted to go and see the horses. I'm going to ask Mom to help me with math, Mom can do anything and I really don't like Sister Theresa. I shouldn't have hateful thoughts about her, I'll just have to tell everything to Father O'Reilly when I go to confession on Saturday". The thoughts rolled through Annie's mind like water pounding the surf.

"You're home early Annie", her mother said as Annie closed the door behind her.

"Yeah", Sister Theresa wasn't there. I waited but she never came".

"Oh, God, I'll have to confess that lie in confession. Father O'Reilly will probably have a heart attack, I've been so bad", thought Annie.

"Don't say yeah Annie, the word is yes".

"Yes, Mom. Mom, can you help me with math? I'm doing better but I think that Sister Theresa is too busy to spend anymore time with me. I'd much rather be at home with you and the boys. Timothy can learn too".

"Well, I think we can do that. I've heard that Sister Theresa has taken on some extra duties. Yes, we can do it, we will start after dinner".

"Thanks Mom, oh, thanks".

And so it started. Math lessons every night after dinner for four months. Mom made it so easy. She put a nickel, a dime, a quarter, a half dollar and a dollar bill on the table.

"A nickel is five, a dime ten, a quarter twenty-five, a half dollar fifty and a dollar one hundred, Mom would say, and Annie caught on like the wind to fire.

" Addition, subtraction and division were a breeze the way Mom explained it. Annie knew she would see an A in math on the Spring exams and she did. No one was more surprised than Sister Theresa.

"Well, it is almost impossible to believe that she got that A without cheating", Sister Theresa said. The dusty chalk residue on the floor powdered the hem of her black habit as she paced back and forth. "It is just impossible to believe. She hasn't had any extra help for four months and she aces the exam. I don't believe it. I insist that she write another exam tomorrow".

Annie sat silently in her chair while Sister Theresa ranted to her father.

Finally, she could take no more. She stood up.

"Why did you call Dad to school? Why didn't you call Mom if you thought I was cheating?" For some reason Annie was very calm. She walked toward the door. She turned.

"I did not cheat on that exam. I will not write another one. My mother has been teaching math to me. She is a really good teacher, better than you. Why do you bother asking my father anything? He knows nothing because he is never at home. He is always with his horses. Why did you call him to the school? I'm going home now."

She was grabbed from behind and flung into a nearby chair. She saw the hand coming down and felt the blow to her face. She moved quickly to avoid the second blow.

"Theresa, for God's sake what are you doing?", Dad shouted.

It was the first time Annie had ever been struck in the face and it would be the only time. John picked up Annie and led her to the car.

"I'm so sorry that happened Annie", he said. "Sister Theresa didn't mean it. She thought you were being disrespectful. I don't think we have to tell your mother about this, it would only upset her".

"Mom will know, Dad. Mom knows everything and I can't lie to her", Annie cried.

"Stop crying, stop crying, your eyes are all red. Oh, God, why did this happen, why did this have to happen now". he said.

Rose was hanging up the telephone as Annie and her father walked through the door.

"Who were you talking to?" John demanded.

"No one important", Rose replied.

She took Annie by the hand and led her into the bathroom. She softly washed her daughter's confused face. As she saw the solid ugly red handprint a rage slowly simmered inside her.

After dinner John left for his horses and Rose went to a meeting.

CHAPTER 4

Baby Joey was now talking and walking. Kate was driving Mom's car and this year would graduate high school. She was planning on entering medical school. "We'll have a doctor in the family", Mom said. But Dad was against it. "Girls become nurses not doctors. It's a waste of money. You'll get married, have your own children and won't work anymore. You can go to nursing school, but not medical school. There will be no more discussion. It's final." Kate spent the next week crying and at the same time making application for nursing school. Dad held the purse strings. How much money he had, nobody knew. He gave Mom a certain amount of money and she paid the bills. "There had to be lots of money", Annie thought. "We live in a big house with two cars and he has his horses, they must cost a lot of money. So, where is the money?"

"Mom, it isn't fair that Kate can't become a doctor. There are other women doctors. Why doesn't Dad want her to be a doctor? There has to be a way. Kate deserves it. She is so smart and is such a good student. I doubt I'll ever be President of Student Council, Editor of the School Paper and everybody loves her", said Annie.

"Don't worry about it, Annie. Kate is going to medical school. She was granted a scholarship."

"It's a miracle, Mom, it's a miracle", Annie cried.

"Believe me Annie, it was no miracle. Never give up on your dreams. If you want something bad enough, go after it, don't ever take no for an answer. If you have the will, there is always a way. Kate worked hard for her scholarship".

"What did Dad say. He won't let her go. I just know he won"t".

"Yes he will. It's settled. Our Kate is going to be a doctor".

"When she becomes a doctor, maybe she will find a cure for Timothy. Maybe he will walk again", Annie cried enthusiastically.

Rose had seen the decline of her first born son. Timothy could do very little for himself now. Every day her heart broke a little more. Such a handsome boy. His big blue eyes always smiled when Rose was near. The hours she spent working on his wasting muscles. Working on his hands so they would remain open but as time went by he was getting weaker and weaker. How much longer would she have him?. He had spent half of his sixteen years of life in a wheelchair and there was nothing she could do to stop the dreaded disease from tearing at his muscles. Rose recalled the exact words of the medical team. "It's an atrophy, a wasting of the muscles". Muscular Dystrophy they called it. She called it hell. .

"Are you okay, Mom, you have a funny look on your face".

"No, I'm fine dear, just thinking about how much I'll miss Kate".

"It will be okay, Mom. I'm here and next year I'll get my learner's permit. I'll be able to drive. I'll run your errands and do your shopping just like Kate. Don't worry, Mom, everything is going to be okay".

The phone was ringing.

"I'll get it", shouted Annie.

"It's for you Mom, its Father O'Reilly".

Rose took the phone.

"Yes, Father, what is it?"

14

"Rose what is going on? I just got word from your husband that Kate will not be attending a Catholic university. When the Catholic Diocese granted Kate a full scholarship, it was to be used to attend St. Mary's. When you met with me, you agreed".

"No, I did not agree. I said there would be no strings attached. I said nothing when St. Mary's was put on the table. You took my silence for consent but in my world silence is not consent. Kate will attend the university of her choice which is McGill and there will be no further discussion".

"You can't do this, Rose".

"I just did and if you take this any further I suggest you recall my visit to you".

"This is blackmail, Rose. You don't have any proof".

"You call it what you want, Father O'Reilly. If you want to put it to the test, go ahead". She hung up the phone.

John was home early.

"I want to talk to you Rose. You had no business going to Father O'Reilly. How did you convince him to award Kate this scholarship? I'm against Kate studying medicine but worst of all is that she will not be going to St. Mary's. Father O'Reilly is on the Board, he can watch out for her. It's a Catholic university with good values right here. She won't have to leave town. I would think you would want her close to home".

"I have nothing against St. Mary's. Kate is eighteen years old. She has attended only Catholic schools, associated only with Catholics and their double standards. I want her to get out in the world, get a sense of who she is and form her own values. You've never taken an interest in Kate. Why now? Afraid of what your friends at the church will think or are you afraid to walk into the next Knights of Columbus meeting? You're more concerned with what people will say than you are about Kate".

"And where is she going to get the money for living expenses? You know the scholarship doesn't cover that. You think you have it all figured out don't you. Well, you don't.

I have no intention of paying any of my money to McGill". His voice was getting louder.

"Lower your voice, John. You are not paying the money to McGill. This is money for Kate to live on. I haven't figured out exactly how much she is going to need each month but I will let you know in due time.

Kate will pay her own bills and learn how to manage her money. If you have a problem with this go talk to your friends, Father O'Reilly and Sister Theresa. I am also enrolling Annie in a private boarding school the next school year. She leaves the same week as Kate", she turned to leave the room.

"Where do you think this money is coming from, Rose? I'm not made of money".

"You have plenty of money. The church sent a statement of your contributions for the past year. It was addressed to both of us so I opened it. I assume it is for tax purposes. You gave the church ten thousand dollars last year. You can cut that in half this next year".

"You can't tell me what to do with my money? Who do you think you are? You're forgetting your place. You're my wife, you take orders from me."

"Go see Father O'Reilly and Sister Theresa. They are probably at the Rectory right now. And let's agree on one thing. From now on you will not interfer with my business. You have your church and your horses. I have my children". She left the room.

John fell into the nearest chair. "What did she know and how much?. Maybe he should start spending more time at home. Was he willing to try? Rose was a good woman. The home she created was the envy of her friends. She was very artistic. When they met they were attending St. Mary's. He was twenty-one years old and she was nineteen. He was in his third year of law and her the first year of arts. Her dream was to be a great artist. She had the talent.

He will never forget the day she told him she was pregnant. They went to Father O'Reilly who married them. Together they told their parents. No one asked if she was pregnant. They just counted the months. Kate was born five months later weighing a mere four pounds. It was a premature birth everyone said. They didn't have to get married. They dropped to their knees in a prayer of thanks. Rose didn't return to school. She devoted herself to the baby and nursed her to health. It was good in the beginning. They lived in a small house that his parents owned. When Kate was three months old Rose got a job at the local Art Gallery to help make ends meet. Her Mother watched Kate. When he graduated with his law degree she was pregnant with Timothy. What a celebration.

He was taken on at the largest law firm in town. Being the low man on the totem pole he worked very long hours. Despite the late hour Rose was always waiting for him. She would warm up his dinner. A plate of homemade spaghetti and a good bottle of Chianti and they would talk about their day while Kate slept. Those were the lean years. If we could only go back. They had very little but they did have each other. How he loved her. She was so petite, he could pick her up with one arm and how she loved to dance. Maybe that's where Annie gets it, he thought. He remembered getting the call at work. Rose was in labor. He remembered rushing to St. Joe's Hospital and holding his son, Timothy, for the first time. Bringing them home. Things gradually changed after that. Rose wasn't always waiting for him. A baby and a two year old. She would be sleeping when he got home. So, rather than go home he would work even later or sometimes he would drop into the Rectory and visit with Father O'Reilly his old friend. They grew up together. Went to the same church, served as altar boys. Tim chose the seminary. He was a good priest. He went on and got his PhD in Psychology. Sometimes when he dropped into the Rectory at night Sister Theresa would also be there, laying out vestments for the morning mass. They were a threesome in high school. How shocked everyone was when she entered the convent. Theresa was a very pretty girl, liked by everyone. Their families were close, always on some committee at church. It was good back then. Everyone thought that he and Theresa would eventually end up together. But he met Rose and loved for the first time. And now here he was thirty-nine years old. He felt he was a good father and husband. The family never lacked for anything. Rose had everything she wanted or did she? It was tough finding out about Timothy and his family didn't help. They had always thought that perhaps Timothy wasn't his. But he knew. Timothy was definitely his son, he could not be denied.

Rose didn't know his exact earnings but could she find out. He kept all tax records at the office and she had never set foot there. He made good money but with the horses and all the extra expenses he had been incurring recently things were getting tight and would be even tighter with Kate at McGill and Annie at boarding school. He would figure a way.

CHAPTER 5

Kate and Annie were both packing for school. Excitement was in the air. Timothy sat in his chair watching as clothes were ironed and folded. Rose had to name tag all of Annie's belongings, a big job with all that Annie wanted to take.

"I've run out of labels", Rose said. "I'll have to run up to the store and get more".

"I'll go", said Kate. "Do you want to come for the ride Annie?"

They backed Rose's car out of the yard and headed for the store.

"I can hardly wait to go to boarding school", said Annie. "I was not looking forward to high school. I'll never be the student you are Kate and the nuns would expect me to be like you. Do you think this is why Mom wants me to go to St.Ann's?".

"I don't know Annie. What I do know is that you are a very special person and I love you. Mom has her reason and I've never known her to be wrong. You are a good student. Why look how you were so determined to get an A in math and you did".

"Yes, I did but I had such a good reason. Dad said if I got an A I could go see the horses. I've never seen them though". She looked out the window and said nothing more.

"Well, let's go see them now. I'm sure Dad will be at the stables. We will stop and phone Mom and let her know we will be longer".

"That would be great. Are you sure? Do you think Dad would mind?", she said.

"Not at all", came the reply.

Kate turned onto the highway and headed for The Acres Stables. The stables were only twenty minutes from home. She had only been there once and promised herself she would never go again but here she was taking Annie.

They entered the gates and drove up a long driveway lined with massive oak trees. The sun was just setting and it seemed so peaceful. She remembered her father's horses were in stable B11. As they rounded the corner Kate saw her father's car parked in his assigned space. She parked next to it.

"You stay here Annie while I go and find Dad".

Kate entered the stable and walked the ten steps to the Tack Room where she knew her father would be and knocked on the door.

The sound of chairs being pushed back, feet hurrying across the floor, the crash of glass.

"It's me Dad, its Kate. I have Annie with me. She wants to see the horses before she goes to school".

"I'll be right there. Just give me a minute", came the reply.

She heard the door unlock and her father stepped out. He pushed his dark, thick hair back into place and smiled, closing the door behind him.

"What a surprise. Does your mother know you're here?, he said.

"Annie is in the car. I'll get her", Kate said curtly.

Annie rushed to her father demanding to see the horses.

"Well, let's start over here, Annie", he said as he took her by the hand.

He showed Annie the dozen horses he had accumulated and pointed out to her the ones that raced and the ones in training. There was a young colt that he had named "Little Annie".

As they walked back towards the car Annie spotted the Tack Room.

"What's in there", she asked.

"Oh, that's where I keep the harnesses and all the other equipment", he said

"Will you show me?. I've never been in a Tack Room".

"Well, there really isn't much to see, Annie".

Kate spoke up. "Go ahead Dad, show Annie what you have in the Tack Room, it won't take long".

John slowly opened the Tack Room door. Annie poked her inquisitive head inside.

"Humm, this is nice. There's a lot of stuff in here. Why you even have a leather couch and other furniture. You could almost live here but what's that smell".

John laughed.

"That's a horsey smell, Annie, now it's time for you and Kate to leave. Your mother will be worried. Tell her I'll be home soon".

He saw his daughters to the car.

As Kate drove away she looked into the rear view mirror. Darkness except for her father standing under the stable lamp. He stood there staring after the car.

"Well, Annie, what did you think of the horses?", Kate asked.

"They are really beautiful but I really don't care if I see them again. I had a funny feeling being there. I didn't like that feeling, it was scary. And the smell bothered me", she said.

"The smell is just the horses. You get used to it when you've been around them awhile".

"No, Kate. It was something else. A familiar smell", Annie said.

As Kate pulled into the driveway they saw Dr. White's car. They both ran into the house. Rose met them and explained that Timothy had a bad spell and couldn't get his breath.

21

Dr. White was calling for an ambulance and Timothy would spend the night in the hospital.

"Now, Kate, I am going to spend the night with Timothy. You and Annie finish up labelling her clothes. Joey is sleeping. Dr. White said this is just a precaution, just being on the safe side. He will be home with us tomorrow", Rose said in a very calm voice but Kate noticed her hands were shaking.

They watched as the ambulance drove away. No siren. No lights.

"They should have put the siren on", said Annie. "Timothy would have liked that".

Timothy didn't come home for a week and when he did a new bed came with him. A bed that Annie could crank up. Rose explained to her that Timothy could breathe better with the head of the bed elevated. So, Annie took on the responsibility of cranking that bed up to the perfect position. It was a really high bed and Annie had to jump up to get on when she read to Timothy which was a daily event during this summer vacation.

CHAPTER 6

"Do you have everything, Annie? Hurry, your father is waiting", Rose shouted.

Annie was saying good-bye to Timothy and she couldn't hold back the tears.

"I really want to go to this school but I'm going to miss you so much, Timothy. I'll write everyday and tell you everything that I'm doing. I'll be home for Christmas". As she hugged him goodbye she felt his thin shoulders.

"I've got to pray harder to God. Timothy isn't getting better. I wonder if God is listening", she thought as she picked up her school bag and ran to the car.

St. Ann's was only a three hour drive from home but it might as well have been in Africa as far as Annie was concerned. It was a big school with 350 girls. As her father drove up the circular drive to the front entrance covered with ivy, Mother Superior appeared. She stood six feet tall with her hands tucked under the heavy white bib of her habit. She wore rimless glasses and wasn't smiling. A young girl was standing next to her. "This is Jeannie and she will take you to the Chapel for afternoon prayers". Annie's enthusiasm was wanning. Right then and there she decided she wasn't going to stay.

"I don't want to stay here, Mom, I want to go back home", she said as she clung to her mother's hand. "Don't make me stay".

Rose bent down and cupped her daughter's face in her hands.

"This is going to be a good experience for you, Annie. You will learn so much here and will make new friends. I've counting on you to give it your best. Now go with Jeannie and I'll see you before we leave.".

In the office Rose and John met the nuns who would be teaching their daughter. After the obligatory tea, chapel prayers had finished and Annie waited outside the office for her parents.

"I'll stay, Mom, but only for this one year. In Chapel I thought about all that you told me about how good this school would be for me. I will do my very best but only for this year. I won't disappoint you", Annie said.

She hugged her parent's goodbye and was escorted to her room. on the second floor. It was a small room with a window, a bed that didn't look too comfortable, a dresser and tiny closet and, of course, a very large crucifix. Someone had placed her trunk in the corner and put the rest of her luggage on top. On the bare dresser was a Daily Schedule.

6:00 am you will rise and make your bed

6:15 morning prayers in your room

6:30 breakfast

7:00 am prayers in the Chapel (do not forget your Chapel veil)

8:00 am Classes begin

Silence. There will be no talking until morning break at 10:15. Silence

As Annie put down the schedule Jeannie was knocking on her door.

"You're really lucky to have a room all to yourself", she said. "It has a window so you'll have lots of company during our free time. Everyone will be in here smoking, blowing the smoke out the window. If we are caught we lose privileges". She opened and closed the window. "Oh, yeah, this is going to be great. You're Dad must have lots of money for you to have your own room. What does he do?", she asked as she took a pack of Black Cat cigarettes from her pocket.

"You can't smoke in my room. I'll get in trouble and I don't want trouble. You have to leave now", Annie said. "Go, I don't want you here".

With a hard push Jeannie slammed open the window and lit a cigarette.

"You listen to me, you little bitch and listen good. There are the school rules and my rules. Mother Superior has put me in charge of looking after you. All new girls are assigned someone and you got me. You're lucky to have me because I can get you all kinds of privileges if you do what I want."

"I want you to leave", said Annie shaking. "You can't smoke here. I will tell Mother Superior".

"You do and you will live to regret it. I will make your time here miserable". She stubbed out the cigarette on the window sill and left.

As Annie started to unpack she wondered, "What do I do now?" She sat on the bed, with folded hands and prayed to God that everything would be okay. "God, are you listening? What do I do? I don't want to be here. I just want to go home". She laid down and sobbing fell asleep.

The harsh ring of the dinner bell woke her. Jeannie was at the door to show her to the dining room. She took Annie by the upper arm and pinched her very hard.

"Did you think about what I told you, you little rat?, she said. "We will be coming to your room after Chapel. You can't lock us out because the doors don't lock around here".

Annie didn't eat much dinner. She didn't know if it was because of Jeannie or the food. It was nothing like Mom's cooking. Who had peanut butter sandwiches and soup for dinner? She never had such a dinner. There was no talking during the dinner hour.

They were led from the dining room to the Chapel for an hour of nightly prayers. As the prayer hour ended Annie spotted Mother Superior and approached her.

"Mother, I've having trouble with the lock on my trunk. Could someone come help me get it open?".

"Of course, Annie, I will be there with Sister Raymond. Just give me ten minutes" she replied.

Annie slowly walked back to her room and waited. Five minutes and there was a knock on her door. Before she could reach it Jeannie came in with Bonnie and Faith.

"Okay, we are here for our nightly smoke. Just shut up. Open the window, Bonnie and let's light up. Shut the door, don't let the smoke out in the hall, those raggedy nuns will be monitoring the hallways pretty soon".

They were well into their smoking when there came a light knock and the door opened. Mother Superior and Sister Raymond entered. A cloud of smoke filled the small room.

The three girls went to the office with Sister Raymond.

"I don't smoke, Mother. Can you have someone else show me around for my first week here? I don't want any trouble. I just want to study hard and go home after this year", she said.

The nun sat down on Annie's bed. Her black habit with the stiff white collar, white crinkled coif that framed her face and the rimless glasses reminded Annie of Sister Theresa but she didn't smell like Sister Theresa. She smelt of wine. "Maybe she spilt some wine at communion", Annie thought.

"Do you know why your parents wanted you to attend this school.", she asked.

Before Annie could reply the nun continued.

"You're here because your mother has to take care of your brother Timothy. He is not getting any better and the doctors don't think he will live much longer. You should pray to God for strength and that he takes him to heaven soon. This is a life lesson for you. He is God's child, just on loan to your parents. You have to face the truth. Now it is time for you to go to bed. Sleep well". She stood up and started to leave.

"I don't believe you", Annie said. "I am not going to sleep. I want to call my mother to come and get me. I'm not staying here".

"You know the rules. You are permitted one phone call every two weeks. That is a priviledge. If you break any rules that priviledge is taken away", she stood up and left.

For the next two weeks Annie spent her free time in study hall and the Chapel. Her challenge was getting back to her room without running into Jeannie and her friends who would push and pinch her at every opportunity while threatening her in a low voice. Finally she was called by Sister Cyrilla, the telephone monitoring nun, that her call home was scheduled for Sunday at 3:00 p.m.

"Don't be a second late or you will not get to make your call", she said. "And I'll be listening in so don't say anything bad or I will cut you off".

Sunday at 3:00 p.m. sharp Annie dialed her home number. The phone rang three time. "Where is Mom", thought Annie. "Surely she is home, she knows I'm calling".

"Hello", Annie heard her mother's sweet voice.

"Mom, it's me, it's Annie.

"Hello, dear, how are you?", she said.

"I'm fine, Mom. I just miss everyone but the girls and Sisters are nice. How is Timothy? Mother Superior told me he is going to die soon. I can't stay here, please come and get me", she cried.

The line went dead.

Sister Cyrilla reached and took the still phone from Annie's shaking hand.

"You will have no privileges for the next three weeks. You will remain silent at all times. You disobeyed me. That is your punishment. Now go to your room and remain there until dinner", she shoved Annie out of the office.

"Mom will be here as soon as she can. I'm not afraid of you. Mother Superior lied to me about my brother. Wait and see, Mom will be here", she slammed the door and left.

Rose called St. Ann's and demanded to speak to Mother Superior. After a long wait she heard the nun's voice.

"What have you told my daughter about her brother's condition", she demanded.

"Oh, Mrs. Thompson, I was just explaining to Annie that eventually we all die and heaven waits for all those who are good. She asked me about her brother and I simply told her that God would call for Timothy when his time was up. Annie is doing just fine here. She has made lots of friend. Please don't worry about her. If she is shows any signs of a deep loneliness I will call you immediately", the nun said in a very friendly way.

"We will be arriving in two weeks to visit Annie and take her to dinner. That is the rule isn't it, Mother Superior or has that changed?, Rose said.

"That is the rule Mrs. Thompson but Annie's privileges have been revoked for the next three weeks because of her disobedience to Sister Cyrilla, so it will be a month before you can come and visit Annie", she said crisply.

"I will be there tomorrow. Have my daughter's belongings packed and waiting in the reception area when I arrive". She hung up the phone.

The next day, true to her word, Rose arrived at the convent. Mother Superior met her. Annie was not in sight nor was her luggage.

"Annie is in the Chapel praying, Mrs. Thompson. We have to talk and then I will get her for you", the nun said arrogantly.

"The hell you will", was the reply.

Rose followed the signs to the Chapel and found her daughter on her knees sobbing. The little white veil that covered her blonde curly head was shaking.

"Come, Annie", she said. "Let's get your stuff, we are going home".

Silently they went to Annie's room, packed up her belongings and headed for the door.

"You realize Mrs. Thompson that you are making a very big mistake. Annie needs discipline and this is the place for her. If she leaves, the yearly tuition will not be returned. I hope you understand that", she said.

"Oh, I am very clear on that. Please call the maintenance man to load this luggage into the car. And by the way, is that wine I smell on your breath? You're a fine one to be talking to me about discipline. I know what goes on here at St. Ann's. I attended this school, as I am sure you remember. I was told things had changed but obviously things have not. I'm taking my daughter home. Let's get out of here, Annie", she said.

On the drive home Annie told her mother everything.

"I know I smelt wine on the nuns. I didn't know what the smell was but I do now and when Jeannie and her friends smoked in my room nothing happened to them. Why was that? I don't understand? ", Annie said.

"I do". Things hadn't changed.

"What's going to happen now, Mom?. Will I have to go back to St. Peter's? I don't want to. Sister Mary Margaret and Sister Theresa are still there. I just can't go back", Annie said.

"You won't have to, Annie. I phoned St. Raphael's and we have an interview with them tomorrow. I have no doubt that you will be accepted. It's across town but arrangements will be made to get you there and home. In a few months you will be sixteen, old enough to drive You can get your learner's permit now and sign up for driving lessons. It will all work out. Don't worry," Rose said.

Annie fell asleep.

The drive home was pleasant. A clear day. Not much traffic but a lot of time for Rose to think. Kate would be off to university, Annie would be at a school that her sister didn't attend. Kate's shoes would be tough for anyone to follow. Such a good daughter and how proud she was of her. From her first grade to the last she excelled. Always at the top of her class but she sure worked for every mark. It was a struggle but she did it.   President of the Student Council, Editor of the school paper, a circle of good friends. Never a moment of worry. Annie, on the other hand, was definitely her own person and had a problem from the beginning with the nuns. She was more interested in her dance classes than school. Now that she was going to high school, a closer eye would have to be kept on her. "I really thought St. Ann's would be the place for her, but I was wrong. Annie has to be free. She can't be locked away in a convent. She needs to be with her family.   John is so doting toward Annie and she adores Timothy. Surprising that John agreed to St. Ann's. Well, he is in for a surprise when he returns from his business trip to find Annie back home. No doubt he thought with Kate and Annie away at school he would have more free time. Well, he could have all the free time he wants.   There was a time when she would wait breathlessly for him to come home. The quiet dinners, the long talks and lovemaking. They were one, so in love, so at peace. The birth of Kate and then Timothy made them a family. And then the heartache of Timothy with a life that would be shortened because of his illness. How cruel life could be. That's when things changed. So much time had to be spent with Timothy and then the birth of Joey. More time taken away from John".

The drive home went by quickly and as Rose pulled into the drive Annie woke.

John's car was there. He and Kate came out to meet them and to bring in Annie's luggage.

"You're back a day early from your trip?, Rose said to John as he reached to help her out of the car.

"The court case wrapped up sooner than expected.   I had a call from Father O'Reilly telling me you were taking Annie out of St. Ann's. He had a call from the convent after you left. I thought it was settled. Annie would stay at St.Ann's".

"Well, she won't be. She is home to stay. I've taken care of matters. Tomorrow we have an interview at St. Raphael's.

Annie ran into the house with Kate to see Timothy. She threw her arms around him and again felt his thinness.

"I'm so glad you're back Annie, I missed you. Mom said you'll be going to St. Raphel's. How do you feel about that?", he said.

"No one knows me there. As much as I love Kate I can't be her so this will be like a new start. They have a wonderful dance program there which is the first class I will sign up for. I'm really excited and Mom said I can get my learner's permit and take driving lessons", she said as she danced around his wheelchair.

John walked in and wanted to know what all the excitement was about.

"Annie is going to get her learner's permit and take driving lessons", Timothy replied.

"Nonsense with the lessons, I can teach Annie how to drive. We can go right now and get your permit and I'll give you your first lesson today". John said. With that they left and drove to the Police Station for the permit and Annie drove home.

"How did you make out?", Timothy cried.

"It's not as easy as it looks. There are so many things to remember. I asked Dad what car I should watch out for and he said to watch the car that's behind the one in front of me. It took me a minute to figure that out. I always noticed when Dad drives that he has one foot on the brake and one on the gas. I did that and he went a little crazy, told me not to do as he does but as he says. It's going to be okay, Timothy, I'll be sixteen in a few months and then I'll get my license. I'll be able to drive back and forth to school. I sure hope that St. Raphael's is nothing like St. Peter's. We'll find out tomorrow", she said.

The interview went much better than Annie expected. She would be accepted into Grade Ten and would start classes tomorrow. No one knew her at this school so it would be a new beginning. Kate would drive her to her first class and it would be the last for awhile as Kate would be leaving for university the next day. How she would miss her big sister. She tried so hard to be like Kate but she was truly the opposite in so many ways.

St. Raphael's. An old established girl's school. Only a selected few were granted entrance and Annie was one of them. As Kate drove up the long circular driveway Annie noticed for the first time the ivy that covered the entrance. There was a peace about this place and for the first time on entering a school Annie felt at home.

Sister Catherine Joseph was waiting for them in the office. As they entered she stood and extended her hand to Annie.

"Welcome, Annie", she said.

Annie reached out for her hand and looked into eyes that were smiling back at her. Despite the coif surrounding the nuns face, Annie saw her beauty. A feeling of happiness and belonging came over Annie. Kate also felt this was the place for her little sister. She would excel here. And excel she did.

Within several months Annie's grades had jumped from low C's to high B's. Sister Catherine Joseph had taken her under her wing and spent a lot of time with her. Annie adored her. But Annie's passion was the dance. She had graduated to hard toe slippers and felt she was floating as she glided over the dance floor. The nuns were amazed at her grace. In only a few months she had transformed herself from a skinny little girl into a young lady with poise and charm. They were in rehearsals for the Christmas pageant and Annie would be the lead ballerina. Annie couldn't believe that she could be any happier. Her sixteenth birthday was around the corner and she would be getting her driver's licence. Driving herself to and from school would be an advantage. She would be able to stay later after school and spend more time with Sister Catherine Joseph. She was sure her Christmas Report would have A's. Low ones but still A's.

The day of the pageant arrived and there was so much excitement in the Thompson house. In the morning Annie practiced her routine over and over for Timothy. He was her best critic. Sister Catherine Joseph had arranged front row seats for the family. Timothy would be right there watching her every step. Kate was home from university on Christmas break so they would all be together. She had driven Kate to school in the early afternoon for one last rehearsal.

"C'mon everyone", Rose said. "We don't want to be late for Annie's performance.

John was carrying Timothy to the car when he went limp in his father's arms.

Turning he rushed back to the house calling for Rose.

"Oh, my God, Rose, what's wrong. My God, help", he cried.

"Lay him on the couch", Rose said calmly..

She loosened Timothy's tie, felt for his pulse and started pounding him on the back; pounding life into him. She looked up into her husband's face and saw a look of hopelessness. Timothy's eyes opened and he coughed.

"What happened, Mom. I had a bad pain and I guess I passed out. Can we still go see Annie? , he mumbled.

"I don't think so, son. I'm going to call Dr. White and have him come take a look at you. John, you take Kate and Joey to the performance. Annie will understand".

She reached for the phone and called Dr. White. He arrived within the hour and checked Timothy. Kate held her son as he fell asleep in her arms. Gently she placed his head on the pillow and she and Dr. White left the room.

"It's not good, Rose. The disease is progressing at a steady rate. The pain Timothy felt was his heart. Statistically, he has lived longer than most afflicted with this dreaded disease. Despite the care and enormous love you have given him, Rose, the day is nearing when the illness will win. You have to prepare yourself", he said gently.

"Can a mother ever prepare herself for her child's untimely death. Even when you know it is inevitable? It is so unfair. Oh how I dread what is to be", she said as she lead the doctor to the front door.

The Christmas pageant was a success. Annie wasn't even aware that her mother and Timothy were not in attendance. After the performance there was a reception for the students and guests but Annie immediately went home to see Timothy. He was sleeping as Annie burst into the house, close to tears.

"How is Timothy, Mom. Is he going to be okay", she cried.

"Yes, Annie, he is going to be fine. He was very disappointed that he didn't see you perform. It is best that we let him sleep through the night. Tomorrow is Christmas Eve and we'll put up the tree. He's looking forward to that. Now tell me everything about tonight. Kate said you dazzled the crowd".

"It was okay, Mom. I didn't want to stay for the reception. As I was rushing out I stopped to say goodbye to Sister Catherine Joseph. There was a woman standing next to her who looked familiar but when I reached them she turned quickly and left. I asked Sister who she was but wasn't given an answer", she said.

"Well, it's getting late, let's all turn in for the night", Rose said as she put her arm around Annie and walked her to her room.

As Rose was putting out the lights, John came to her and said he was going to the office to finish some work.

CHAPTER 7

Annie was counting the weeks and then days until her sixteenth birthday. The Shadow Villa was contracted to cater the party. Annie and her mother had chosen the menu to be served, the decorations and the music. Programs were printed and were enclosed with the invitations. There would be 120 people there. Most of them Annie wouldn't even know. A lot were business associates of her father's, relatives Annie hadn't seen for years but relatives that were connected and of course everyone from the church. Annie had a small group of friends and they would all be there. Annie's dress was an ivory peau de sois with a bright turquoise sash. Her platinium hair was pulled back in a Gibson style and held in place with small ribbons the color of her sash. It would certainly be an evening to remember.

Annie made her entrance on her father's arm. Everyone applauded.

Father O'Reilly blessed the party and wished Annie well. As he raised his hand in blessing he took a second look at Annie and knew she was no longer a little girl with a bad eye defect but a beautiful young woman. The beautiful gown she was wearing accented the curves of her perfect body. The boys will be pounding down her door, he thought. John had better keep a close watch over her.

Timothy was never far from Annie's sight. She glanced across the room at him and was stunned to see how thin he had become. He seemed to be leaning to the side of his wheelchair. She walked toward him and asked if he was having a good time. He looked up and smiled. "I always have a good time when you're close by, Annie. You really are beautiful. Who was that good looking fellow you were dancing with a short while ago? The tall good looking fellow in the dark suit.?, he asked.

"Oh, that is Mark Cohen. He is the son of one of Dad's partners. I really like him because he is a great dancer. He knows how to do the twist - the latest dance craze. Dad would have a fit if we ever did it here. When we get home I'll show you how it's done. I just bought the record by Chubby Checker. C'mon I'll introduce you to Mark. He's a nice guy".

The party was a roaring success and as grateful as Annie was she was more excited to get her driver's license the following day. She was to meet her father at the police station for the driving test. It was a breeze she later told Timothy. It was a pretty exciting week for Annie but there was more to come. After dinner that night Rose and John told her there was another surprise. As she had done so well in the tenth grade, not only aceing Math but 90% of all her subjects there was yet another gift for her waiting outside. Annie looked around for Timothy but he was no where to be seen. They lead her outside with her eyes covered with a silk scarf. The scarf was removed and there before Annie was a new covertible car with Timothy sitting in the front seat. Annie burst into tears and hugged her mother and then her father. She ran to the car and jumped in the front seat and hugged her brother.

"We are going to have the summer of our lives, Timothy. You just wait and see. I can't believe this. I'm so happy".

And it was a summer to remember. From the day school got out Annie and Timothy were inseparable. A series of belts were installed on the passenger side of Annie's car that would hold Timothy in place. A rest for his head was installed on the back of his seat. With all this in place Timothy sat up straight in the car with his head stable. Despite everything that had been done for Timothy's comfort as the summer days passed each became shorter and shorter as he tired very quickly. On one of their last summer days Annie decided to take Timothy to see their father's horses. It had been a long time since she was at the stables but felt pretty confident she would be able to find them. She knew her father wouldn't be there in the afternoon but she was pretty sure the man who kept guard for her father would recognize her.

As she made the turn into Acres Stables she remembered the long driveway lined with the oak trees but she couldn't remember the number of the stable. Well, she would just drive around until she recognized it. Turning a corner she recognized the stable and parked in front was her father's car.

It was very quiet and Annie wondered if her father was here or over at the race track. She approached the door and knocked. No answer. She lifted the latch and pulled the door open and stepped inside.

"Hello. Dad are you here?", she called. There was no answer. The Tack Room door was ajar. Annie pushed it open and as she did she saw the shadow of a woman and man embracing. Who were these people, Annie thought and what were they doing in Dad's Tack Room. She turned to leave, closing the door. A familiar smell. She kicked the door open and screamed for her father. From behind her arm was grabbed.

"What's all the hollering about, Annie?", her father said. "What are you doing here?

"I brought Timothy to see the horses. What are you doing here? I thought you would be at work and who was that woman in the Tack Room that you were hugging?".

"Don't be silly, Annie, there is no woman here. You probably just saw shadows of the saddles and bridles. You have such an imagination. Now, let's bring Tim in and show him around".

Timothy loved everything about the horses. The smell of the oats, the leather saddles, the rubdown linament, the horses themselves. Too soon it was time to go. John put Timothy in the car, secured him with the belts, folded the wheelchair and put it in the truck of Annie's car.

"Are you going to leave the top down, Annie?. It looks like it may rain", her father said. Annie didn't reply. Perhaps she should have listened, Annie thought. Half way home the clouds burst open and sheets of rain fell. She scrambled to get the top up and wiped the rain off Timothy. "How I hate the rain", she thought. "Someday I will live where the sky is always sunny and blue and I will take Timothy with me. Just two more years of school and then I will be going to university. A university far from this rainy city".

"Annie, it's wonderful to see you", Sister Catherine Joseph greeted Annie at the convent door. "I was surprised and delighted to receive your call but what could be so urgent that you had to see me this evening?.

She led Annie into the reception area of the convent. It was very ghostly to Annie. The high 20' ceilings, the echo of your footsteps as you walked across the wooden floors and everyone whispered. It was too quiet. Votive candles in ruby red containers burned with barely a flicker of the flame.

"Sit here, Annie", Sister Catherine Joseph said. "What has got you so worried".

"Sister, I think my father is cheating on my mother. I took Timothy to the stables today and Dad was there when he should have been at work. I saw the shadow of a woman hugging him although Dad said it was my imagination. That it was the shadows of the tack room that I saw. But I know differently. And there was a smell that was so familiar to me. I can't place it but I know that smell. I don't know what to do? Should I tell Mom?".

"Oh, Annie. Your father would never cheat on your mother. He is a good Catholic man who lives by the doctrines and commandments of the church. You must never think that. What you saw had to be shadows. Did you ask your father why he was at the stables in the afternoon?".

"Yes", Annie replied. "He said he came out to check on one of the horses that was not very well."

"Well, that's it. Now, you just get all those thoughts out of your mind and start thinking about the year ahead of you. Grade Eleven is not easy but I will be there to give you all the extra help you need. Your marks are in the top five percent let's keep them there. Why at this rate, you could easily be the Valedictorian of your graduating class next year. You will also have to start thinking about your university. I am sure you will have your pick, you are doing so well. Hopefully, you will choose St. Mary's unlike your sister. Father O'Reilly was very upset with Kate for going to McGill but I understand she is doing very well there. You must also think about joining the CYO this year. They have some wonderful programs and a dance every Friday night. Father Leary is in charge of the dances. Now don't you worry about your father. He is a good man, Annie.

I'll see you in a few weeks for the start of the school year. As she reached to hug Annie there was a very sad look in her eyes. "I should believe Sister Catherine Joseph", thought Annie, "but I know something isn't right. I'll phone Kate, she will know what to do".

That evening Annie tried to reach Kate but with little success. As she placed the telephone receiver in the cradle the phone rang.

"Hello", said Annie.

"Hello Annie, this is Mark Cohen. I was wondering if you would like to go out this Friday night? There is a dance at the Lily Pavillion. It is a very nice place on the lake. It wouldn't be a late night, I would have you home by midnight".

"Mark, I would love to go. I've heard about that Pavillon but don't you have to be eighteen to get in?".

"Yes, you do, but this is a special dance for sixteen to eighteen year olds to celebrate the end of summer vacation", he said.

"I will ask Mom and get back to you. Thanks for calling", Annie said as she hung up the phone and went to Timothy.

"Do you remember that fellow I introduced you to at my party? Mark Cohen. Well, Timothy, he just called and invited me to a dance at the Pavilion this Friday night. I'm excited. I hope Mom says it's okay to go. I've got to go ask her now. Say a prayer for me", she whispered as she went in search of her mother.

"Why, yes, I remember Mark. His father works at the law firm. A very nice boy. It's fine with me, Annie, but we should also talk to your father about this. He will be home shortly for dinner and you can ask him then. He still thinks you're too young to date but he may make an exception this time because he knows Mark's father", Rose said with a smile.

At dinner that night Annie blurted out that Mark had asked her to a dance.

John put down his fork in utter surprise.

"You can't go out with Mark Cohen. For God's sake, Rose, what were you thinking when you said it was alright with you. Mark Cohen is a Jew. You can't date a Jew, Annie. No, I will not have it and there will be no discussion on the subject". He left the table, grabbed his keys and went out the door.

Annie got up from the table, walked to the phone and called Mark Cohen.

"Hello, Mark", she said. "This is Annie and I would love to go to the dance with you Friday night".

"Annie, are you sure you're doing the right thing. Your father will never forgive you", said Rose.

"Forgive. He should be asking my forgiveness. How dare he preach to me about treating people equally. Be a good Christian, he says. He can go to confession and communion, pound the good book but he is a hypocrit. How dare he. He's a fine one to talk".

Mark picked Annie up at 8:00 o'clock Friday night. Dressed in a powder blue dress with her hair tied back with silver ribbons, she was a vision.

Earlier Timothy voiced his concern.

"Oh, Annie, if Dad finds out you will be grounded for life", he said. "You have never disobeyed him, why now?"

"Because he is wrong, Timothy. He is very wrong. I'll be home by midnight, as I promised Mom. Don't you worry. I'll tell you all about it in the morning".

The Lily Pavillon on the Lake was beautiful. Annie and Mark joined his friends and danced the night away. Mark really knew how to do the twist and taught Annie a few new steps. She was elated. On the drive home Annie asked Mark if he would like to go to the horse races the next day.

"I've never been to the races", she said. "I know Dad races his horses in the afternoon. I'm going to take Timothy. He has never seen a race. I think it's about time".

The following day Mark arrived at Annie's house.

"We will take my car", said Annie. "It has a special harness for Timothy. You wll have to sit in the back, Mark, I hope you don't mind and I've put the top down. Timothy likes the wind blowing on his face".

Mark was very tall and strong for his eighteen years. He gently picked up Timothy from his wheelchair, placed him in his seat and helped Annie with the straps. He then put the folded chair in the trunk.

"Amazing", thought Annie. "I didn't have to tell him what to do. He instinctively knew how to help with Timothy".

"And they're off", the announcer shouted as Annie and Mark got Timothy as close to the fence as possible.

"Which one is Dad's?", Timothy asked.

"The jockey wearing the brown and yellow colors. He's riding Jeannie Brown and is in third position. Here they come around the final turn, Timothy. He's moving up and I think they may just win".

Sure enough Jeannie Brown placed first.

Annie looked toward the winner's circle and saw her father. Standing beside him was a woman who was looking up at him smiling.

"That's the woman", Annie thought. "Who is she, she looks so familiar but I can't place her".

They stayed for two more races and left as Timothy was getting very tired.

CHAPTER 8

The start of a new school year. Annie couldn't believe that she was in grade eleven and her little brother Joey would be starting the first grade.

"Welcome back, Annie", Sister Catherine Joseph said as she reached out and hugged her. "Did you have a wonderful summer?. You must tell me all about it but now let me show you to your homeroom. You will be in my Math and English class. You have Sister Maria Rose for all the others".

Entering the classroom Annie saw that most everyone from grade ten was there. It was a fine reunion and chatter about their summers was interrupted by Sister Catherine Joseph who brought the class to attention and outlined the curriculum for the year.

"Girls", she said. "This is a very important year. At the end of this school year you have just one more year of high school and you must start thinking ahead regarding where you would like to attend a university".

And so the eleventh year of school began.

Annie had a different attitude. She couldn't put her finger on it; was it because her grades had drastically improved last year, was it because she was now sixteen years old and feeling very good about herself or was it because she was dating Mark Cohen and only Timothy and her mother knew. It wasn't that they saw a lot of each other but the time they did spend together Annie really enjoyed. Mark was fun to be with and most of all he knew how to dance.

Annie was now in her tenth year of studying ballet and she looked so forward to her first class but her grades had to improve even more if she was to gain entrance to a top university. She had every intention of studying for her Law Degree. She knew her father would not approve but she didn't really care.

During the first day of school Sister Catherine Joseph took Annie aside and laid out for her the days and time for tutoring in Math and English. "These subjects are extremely important", she told Annie. "We will build up your grades and you will have no problem getting into St. Mary's University. In fact, you may even qualify for a scholarship. Have you given any thought to what you may want to study? Your father told me that you would no doubt be studying for your teacher's degree?"

Annie smiled and said, "I'll decide when the time is right".

Three weeks later Annie received a call from Father O'Leary.

"Annie, the CYO Council is having their first meeting to elect members . I would really like you to attend and run for President. We will be meeting Wednesday night at six o'clock and I expect you to attend", he said and before Annie could reply he hung up.

She immediately phoned him back.

Before he could say anything, Annie told him she would not be attending the meeting, she had no intention of running for President and thanked him for considering her.

Before he could reply she hung up the phone with a smile on her face knowing full well his next call would be to her father and right she was.

At dinner that evening her father was not in a good mood. Annie kept up idle chatter with her mother and Timothy waiting for her father to explode and explode he finally did.

"What is going on with you, Annie", he said. "I had a call from Father O'Reilly today. He told me he wanted you to run for President of the CYO and you refused. What good reason could you possibly have?, he demanded.

"I don't want to run for President. I will attend the dances but I don't have time. I would rather spend my time studying, taking my dance classes and being home.

There are lots of others who would love to be President and would do a better job than I. It doesn't matter what you or Father O'Reilly want I won't do it. I don't like Father O'Reilly and want as little to do with him as possible. Just because he is a priest doesn't mean I have to like him".

Everyone at the table was shocked at Annie's words.

Pushing her chair back, she excused herself from the table and went to her room.

"What in the name of God has got into your daughter", he demanded of Rose. "I don't even know her anymore. She is to be grounded, take her car away and all privileges. She is totally out of control. How dare she speak to me that way". He threw down his serviette, grabbed his keys and left the house.

Timothy burst out laughing.

"She sure isn't like the rest, Mom", he said. "She sure isn't like the rest".

Little Joey spoke up and said, "I want to be like Annie when I grow up".

And so the school year started. Joey began following Annie around like he was her shadow. No privileges were taken away. Rose was in charge of her children.

CHAPTER 9

Kate was coming home for a visit. Just one more year of study and she would be a doctor. Annie was so excited. Letter and phone calls were great but to have her home again was the real charm.

Annie picked Kate up at the airport and on the ride home brought Kate up on all the news. School was great particularly with the extra help from Sister Catherine Joseph. Her only worry was Timothy. He wasn't getting any better and was so thin. "My world will fall apart if anything happens to Timothy", Annie cried to Kate.

"Only God knows how long Timothy will be with us", Kate said. "We may have him for years or maybe only months but when the time comes for Timothy to leave we will be strong and know that he will be in a better place".

"I don't believe that", said Annie. "I'll never believe that".

But Kate knew it was only a matter of time. During her studies she spent hours researching the horror of this disease. If they had Timothy for another year, two at the most it would be a miracle.

Annie pulled into the driveway honking her horn. Rose ran to her elder daughter and hugged her. How wonderful it was to have Kate home. The table was set for a celebration dinner. The crystal, china and sterling were brought out in

Kate's honour. After dinner Kate and her mother went for a walk.

"How are you really doing, Kate", her mother asked. "Are you happy in your chosen field?

"It has been a rewarding struggle, Mom", she said. "Another year and I will graduate. I will then come home and do an internship at the General Hospital. My concern is for Timothy. How is he doing, Mom.

Tears started to well up in Rose's eyes.

"He isn't doing well, Kate. Everything possible has been done. I know it is just a matter of time but that is so hard to accept. I am just taking one day at a time, expecting the worst but hoping for the best".

They walked back to the house arm in arm to find Annie in her ballet tights, tutu and satin hard toed slippers performing for Timothy and Joey. They all applauded.

Everything seemed so normal but Rose knew different. Kate home for a visit but her father wasn't there to greet her. What was so important that he failed to show up. Annie didn't seem surprised that he wasn't there. Kate never mentioned the absence of her father.

The following day Kate met with her old school friends for a small reunion. It was good to know she had not been forgotten. Margaret, who had been her closest friend all through school, was now married with a small child.

"Who is the special man in your life, Kate", she asked.

"I don't have too much time for dating, she replied, but there is a man I've been seeing. He is a fellow student and plans to specialize in Paediatrics. His name is Tom Gallagher and he is from Boston".

"Sounds like he would be quite a catch but then again so would you", she said.

Kate laughed. "I didn't go to McGill to meet a husband, Margaret. I went to study to be a Doctor. Tom is just a good friend. Marriage is not in the cards for me at this time. I have much more to do before I ever settle down".

"Speaking of marriage", Margaret said as she took a sip of her wine, "how are your parents?"

"Oh, they are fine. I haven't seen Dad yet. He wasn't at home last night. At a meeting I understand but I'll see him tonight.

Margaret looked up into Kate's eyes and thought she doesn't know. She has been gone too long to know.

When Kate arrived home her father was waiting for her.

"How is our future Doctor" he said. He made no move to hug her. "It is great that you have done so well and achieved such good marks. Do you have any plans yet for when you graduate. Will you be coming home?"

Kate explained to him that she would be coming home. As she surveyed her father she knew something had changed. He seemed agitated and wanting to leave.

"Well, it is good to have you home, Kate, as brief as your visit will be", he said.

The telephone rang and he quickly reached for it. After a few brief words, he hung up the phone and said he had to leave. There was a problem at the stables with one of his horses.

"Well, I'll come along", Kate said. "I may not be a horse doctor but I may be able to contribute something".

Her father abruptly said no and left.

Fortunately, Annie was at home and Kate asked to borrow her car.

"Of course", Annie said as she handed her sister the keys. "Where are you going. Would you like company?"

"No, Annie, I won't be long" and she left.

As Kate started up Annie's car she saw the tail lights of her father's car at the end of the driveway. He took a left which surprised Kate as the stables were to the right.

She followed very carefuly but believed her father was not thinking about being followed. She traveled cautiously behind her father for several miles. He signaled to turn left and his car disappeared. Kate pulled up to the entrance of a small but lovely Cape Cod style house just as her father was greeted by a tall, dark-haired woman who reached up and kissed him.

She sat there for a long time not stunned or even surprised. She had a feeling that her father was having an affair. He was never home when she called nor was he ever mentioned in her conversations with Annie and her mother and why would her friend Margaret ask about her parent's marriage. Well, she now had the answer.

Turning the car around she drove slowly home with warm tears flowing from her green eyes. Did her mother know? They say the wife is always the last to know but her mother was not like the others. She must know.

Entering her home, Kate found her mother reading to Timothy and Joey. Annie was doing her school assignments.

Rose looked up as Kate came into the parlor. Joey was almost asleep and Kate reached for him and carried him to bed. Going back to her mother Kate looked over at Timothy and he was looking very pale and tired.

"Are you also ready to call it a night, Timothy?", she asked.

"I am tired but I have to wait for Dad to come home and lift me into bed", he replied.

"Nonsense, I can do that. Mom can help. It is no problem and remember I'm almost a doctor so I know how to lift people without hurting myself. C'mon Mom, lets get Timothy into bed and we should also call it an early night", Kate said.

A half hour later Kate, Annie and their mother were having a goodnight cup of tea.

"Well, Annie", Kate said. "You have only two more years of school. Do you have any thoughts as to what you want to do when you graduate?"

"I want to go to law school. I know Dad will not approve but that's what I want to do", she said so full of confidence.

Kate and Rose laughed together.

"Since when did your father's objections ever bother you", her mother said.

"I think it is a wonderful plan and have you thought about what university you want to attend?", Kate said.

"Well, I know McGill has a very good faculty but I'm also thinking about the University of Toronto and then Osgoode Hall", Annie replied. "I have another year to decide but Sister Catherine Joseph said I have to get my marks up. She thinks I'm going to take teaching at St. Mary's. That's what Dad told her. I don't know why he would say that because I have never talked to him about it. As a matter of fact I rarely talk to him about anything lately. He is always gone".

Kate said they should all turn in and have a goodnight's sleep. She only had tomorrow at home and wouldn't be back until after graduation.

John came home to a quiet, dark house. He turned around and left locking the door behind him. Rose heard the door open and close and she waited. Soon she realized he had left and she silently cried for what should have been. "I do love him. I should make an effort to spend time with him but the children take up so much of my time".

CHAPTER 10

Three weeks into school and a notice was posted on the bulletin board. The first CYO dance would be in two weeks. Annie was looking forward to it. She would invite Mark and introduce him to her friends. He was such a nice guy and so polite. He had never made a move toward Annie and God help him if he did. Annie was too involved with other important matters to get involved with anyone romantically. She would rather be at home.

At dinner that night Annie told her mother her plans.

"The first CYO dance is in a couple of weeks, Mom, and I am going to invite Mark. He can meet my friends and I know we will have a good time", Annie said.

"Oh, Annie, that is not a very good idea. You father will find out that you have been seeing Mark and life will be unbearable", Rose said.

"I don't care, Mom. Dad is never around, too busy with his horses. I really don't think he cares that much about us. It is all about friends at church. He is probably more concerned with what other people think than he is about us.

I don't care, I just don't care", Annie said as she ran her fingers through her long blonde hair.

Rose looked over at her daughter and silently applauded her for seeing some people for what they were. She had turned into a beautiful young sixteen year old. Wasn't all that interested in where the boys were and Rose liked it that way. The friends that Annie did bring home were given a once over by Timothy. If he didn't think they were suitable friends, Annie never saw them again. How could Timothy be so insightful. A young man whose life was bound to a wheelchair but who had a good sense about people. And how he adored Annie. She brought him into her life and shared everything with him.

During the next two weeks at school the talk was all about the first CYO dance. What would everybody be wearing and who would be their date? Annie didn't mention her date and hadn't decided what to wear. She would shop this weekend for a new outfit. Maybe Mom could have someone sit with Timothy and Joey and come with her. Annie was getting excited. It would be a lot of fun.

Rose did make arrangements to have a friend stay with the boys while she and Annie went shopping. They decided on a emerald green skirt and ivory blouse. The skirt had several crinolins and when Annie twirled around the skirt flowed with her. Patent leather pumps completed the outfit and she would wear her hair down.

The afternoon of the dance Mark called to say he would not be able to pick Annie up because of a family commitment but he could meet her there at 10:00 pm. Annie was fine with that.

"Don't worry, Mark," she said. "I will meet you at the entrance at 10:00 pm", Annie said.

The night of the dance Annie was dressed and looked beautiful as she came into the room where Timothy was waiting for her.

"Oh, Annie, you look perfect. Lucky Mark. Remember every detail and tell me all about it tomorrow", said Timothy.

Annie drove herself to the dance and thought why couldn't Timothy come to the CYO dances? He would enjoy watching everyone. The next dance Timothy will be my date if Mom says its okay.

Annie parked her car and walked toward the building. A hugh banner was waving in the breeze. "Welcome to the Catholic Youth Organization's Dance", it read.

Father O'Mally was greeting everyone as they entered.

Annie didn't know him, he must be new, she thought. He extended his hand in welcome to Annie and said, "You must be Annie Thompson. I know your father very well, we went to school together. Your father told me you would be coming tonight but he didn't tell me what a beautiful daughter he had".

Annie smiled and shook his hand. He held her hand a little too long in Annie's opinion. Another priest she wasn't going to like. As Annie looked toward the ballroom she spotted her friends and excused herself from Father O'Mally.

The room was decorated in fall colors with hugh bouquets of autumn leaves and flowers. It was magnificent. There had to be at least 150 students here. The girls from three different Catholic schools and the boys from St. Michael's. Annie spotted her closest friend, Nancy, who was standing with a group of girls from her school.

"Oh, Annie, I'm so glad you're here. You can show us how to do the Twist. No one dances better than you", Nancy said.

The music started up and Annie proceeded to show Nancy and her new friends how to do the Twist and the music played continuously. Father O'Mally approached the group of girls and took Annie aside.

"There is someone I would like you to meet, Annie. He is a grade twelve student at St. Michael's. I think you will like him", he said. "Come over here Bill and meet Annie Thompson".

Annie was introduced to Bill Nash and after talking with him for a few minutes realized they had nothing in common. She looked at her watch and the time was ten pm.

Excusing herself she went to the entrance hoping that Mark would be there. The entrance was crowded with people still coming in. In the middle of the line she spotted him.

Walking toward him, smiling she reached out for his hand and said, "come this way, Mark. I'm so glad you are here". Together, hand in hand they went into the dance.

No sooner had they started dancing when Father O'Mally interrupted them and took Annie aside.

"Annie, this dance is for members of the CYO and your guest is going to have to leave", he said.

"Mark is my guest and just because he is not a Catholic is no reason to make him leave", Annie said indignantly. "If he leaves then I leave and I won't be back. Is this the way the CYO treats guests of a different faith? How hypocritical can you be?". She turned on her heel, took Mark's hand and with head held high walked out of the CYO.

Outside Annie apologized to Mark. Mark leaned over and kissed Annie on the cheek.

"Don't fret about it, Annie. This has happened to me before. There are places where Jewish people are not welcome. The golf club that your father belongs to, my father can't. It isn't right but that's how it is and I've grown to accept it. Can I call you tomorrow and maybe we can see a movie?" He kissed her again on the cheek and they said goodnight.

Fuming Annie drove home, burst through the door and told her mother what happened. She didn't realize her father was in the other room.

"Can you believe it, Mom. That awful Father O'Mally said Mark couldn't stay at the dance. It wasn't because he didn't belong to the CYO, it was because he was Jewish. I just can't believe it. And do you know the golf course Dad belongs to, Mark's father can't join because he's Jewish. Why would Dad belong to a club where they show prejudice against people of a different religion. Dad can't know about this. He wouldn't belong to such a club. Would he Mom?".

Rose reached out for her daughter and wiping away her tears thought her Annie has had her first taste of the real world. She looked up and John was standing in the doorway.

"I thought I told you you weren't to see Mark Cohen. If you had listened to me none of this would have happened.

You don't listen. You just go off and do whatever you want regardless of the consequences. I hope you have learned your lesson".

Annie stood up and glared at her father.

"Oh, yes I've learned Dad. I've learned that Father O'Reilly, Father Sullivan and Father O'Mally are nothing but hypocrites. They preach to us about being good Christians, helping our fellowman, treating people equally but yet a good Jewish person is asked to leave a sacred Catholic building and then I find out that my own father belongs to a club where Jews are not permitted. Don't talk to me ever again about how I should act around other people. You and your buddies at the rectory could take a lesson from me. I will never go to the CYO again and if I didn't like Sister Catherine Joseph so much I would refuse to attend a Catholic school and there is nothing you can do about it. How could I have a father who is against different people. What do they say at your church about Timothy? He's different. He can't walk. Remember they wouldn't even let him go down the aisle with me when we received our First Communion. Yea, they are real Christians, Dad. You must be real proud to be part of them. They make me sick. They are nothing but a bunch of two-faced bastards". She left the room.

John stood silently, speechless. He finally spoke.

"Rose, you had better get her under control", he said.

"It should be humbling to you, John. To have your daughter teach you a lessson in what's right and wrong. Annie is right. She was wrong in the name calling but right in everything else. Father O'Mally had no right whatsoever to insult Annie and Mark by asking him to leave and you know it. I have taught Annie to accept people for who they are, not to judge them on their religion or race. I've done a good job. Now I am going to go to Annie and tell her how proud I am of her".

John picked up his car keys and left.

When Rose went to Annie's room she wasn't there. She found her sitting on Timothy's bed telling him all about the disastrous evening.

"I'm not wrong Timothy", she was saying. "If Dad doesn't quit the golf club then he is just like the rest of them".

"It will be okay, Annie, it will be okay. Don't worry. Just be yourself and don't judge. Don't judge Dad. He lives in his world of work, his horses and his friends at the church. He doesn't have much else. Now go make some tea, Mom will sit me up and we will have a cup before you go to bed. Are you going to the movies with Mark tomorrow?", Timothy asked.

"Yes I am. Would you like to come along? It's a western, I know you will like it," Annie said.

"If I'm feeling up to it, Annie. We'll see tomorrow. Now go make the tea".

CHAPTER 11

Sister Catherine Joseph was waiting for Annie on Monday morning. She had rehearsed what she was going to say to her and hoped that she could get through to her.

Annie arrived at school early.

"Come to my office, Annie", Sister Catherine Joseph said. Before she could say another word, Annie said,

"If you want to talk to me about what happened at the dance Friday night, before you do I have a question for you.

Do you believe it is right that Jewish people or anybody else of a different religion should not be admitted to certain clubs or organizations? If you cannot answer me with a yes or no then we have nothing to talk about. If it wasn't for you I would not be coming to this school. I can't be with people who don't believe as I do, so maybe it is better that you don't answer and we won't talk about it. You are the only one outside of my family that I can talk to and who I trust. I don't want to lose you. My friend Mark's school is having their dance next Saturday. I will be going with him. Do you think they will ask me to leave? For some reason, I doubt it".

And so the school year continued. Dad remained a member of the golf club. Annie spent more time at home.

CHAPTER 12

The invitations were out for Kate's graduation. Other than Timothy the family would be going to Montreal for the event. There would be a big reception at the Shadow Inn when Kate came home. Two days before they were to leave Timothy was rushed to the hospital because he couldn't breathe.

Rose was at his bedside thinking that she would not be going to Montreal. She wanted to go for Kate but did not want to enter the city where her son was diagnosed with Muscular Dystrophy. As though reading her thoughts, Timothy said, "Mom, you don't have to stay with me. I will be alright. Kate needs you there. Go Mom. I want you to go.

And don't tell Kate I'm back in the hospital. She will just worry".

Annie was also there.

"Timothy is right, Mom. You have to go but I don't. Kate will understand why I want to stay with Timothy. She knows I don't like it when we have to leave him. I will be here everyday after school and will stay until they kick me out at eight pm. Kate will be home in two weeks and we will celebrate at her party.

Rose gave in to Annie as she normally did. The following day Rose, John and Joey left for Kate's graduation. It was a beautiful convocation. Rose explained to Kate that although Annie wanted to be there she was coming down with a bad cold and it wasn't wise for her to fly. Kate accepted the explanation but believed there was more to it.

True to her word, Annie was at the hospital for the next two days. They were the best days she and Timothy shared since the summer she got her car. But during those days Annie realized that Timothy would never get well. That everyone was right. That maybe they wouldn't have him very much longer. But in her mind she never gave up hope for if she gave up on hope then all is lost. She loved her older brother so much it hurt to see him growing weaker and weaker.

Two days later Kate came home with the family. They went straight to the hospital to find Annie sitting up on Timothy's bed reading to him. He was lying there very listless, half asleep. "Timothy, it's Kate. We are all back from Montreal". Joey sat at the foot of the bed next to Annie. Timothy opened his eyes and smiled at Kate.

"Congratulations, Doctor. I am so proud of you and really happy that you are back home to stay. It has been a long time since my family has been in the same room together".

Kate noticed that his breathing was very labored yet there was no breathing apparatus by his side. His private nurse came into the room. It was time for them to leave.

"We will be back tomorrow morning to take you home, Timothy. I'm sure Dr. White will agree that we can certainly take care of you at home", Kate said.

An hour later Kate and Rose were having tea. Joey and Annie had gone to bed. John left from the hospital to go to the stables.

"How are you doing, Mom? You seem to have accepted that Timothy will not be with us much longer. How do you feel, what are you thinking?", Kate asked.

"I worry a lot about what will happen when we lose Timothy. I know it is inevitable but so hard for me to accept. Annie has one more year of school and then she will be gone. I worry more about her because of her closeness to Timothy. And that will just leave Joey at home. Perhaps I will go back to my painting. But for now it is just one day at a time for me. And you, Kate, what about you? When you finish your internship do you plan on moving on or staying here?", Rose replied.

"I have time to think about that, Mom. I haven't mentioned Tom to you but I've been seeing a lot of him and he plans on moving here and setting up practice. He is a pediatrician and I think I'm in love with him. You will like him. He is a good man, kind, compassionate and with a great sense of humor which has pulled me out of my doldrums on more than one occasion. He will be arriving here within the month. I'm anxious for you to meet him".

The next day Timothy came home with a breathing apparatus. Having Kate at home would take a lot of pressure off of Rose. The equipment was set up next to his bed and Kate gave Annie and her mother instructions on its use should Timothy get short of breath again. Hopefully, this would eliminate trips to the hospital. Rose felt a sense of security having the equipment so close. She would be able to help Timothy if and when needed. Annie, although she didn't say anything, wasn't too happy about it. This just meant that Timothy wasn't ever going to get better. He could do less and less for himself and he was so thin. Each day Annie's heart broke a little bit more.

CHAPTER 13

"Well, Annie, we are coming into the home stretch", said Sister Catherine Joseph.

"Home stretch", thought Annie. "That's a racing term. What could Sister ever know about horse racing".

"In just two months", she continued "summer vacation will be here and then just one more year of high school for you. Give a lot of thought to what you want to do when you graduate. In the spring, if your marks continue to improve, you should get a scholarship to St. Mary's. I know you can do it. I am so proud of your accomplishments".

During that summer Annie spent her time between dancing classes and staying at home with Timothy. There were no outings in the convertible, no movies or horse races. He was just too weak. With Kate at home bedtime came earlier and earlier for him. It was so good having Kate home. She took charge of Timothy's medical needs. A wonderful help for Rose. When Timothy was resting Annie spent her time with Joey. What an adorable little boy. Big brown eyes with a full mop of hair. He was so inquisitive, wanting to know everything. Annie took him to the library, museums and to the campus of St. Raphael's. He would be going into grade two and "someday", he would say "I'll be going to university just like you Annie".

The final year of school was starting for Annie. Her friend Mark would be leaving for the university in two weeks to study medicine. She would miss her friend. He was always there to pick up Annie's spirits when she was feeling low. Yes, she would indeed miss him.

This year would be nothing but hard study for Annie. She was determined to get a scholarship. Sister Catherine Joseph would continue to tutor her after school.

In early spring, the grade twelve students were given a list of universities and their requirements along with applications for scholarships. Annie was only interested in The University of Toronto and she felt very confident she would be accepted.

Finals exams would be written in April and graduation was scheduled for May 30th. There was to be a prize for the English essay and the student with the top grades would be Valedictorian. She knew Janet Lewis would have that top honor. Janet had honors all through high school and she deserved it. Annie had admired Janet all through school.

For two weeks prior to the finals Annie rarely surfaced from studying. "You can do it, Annie", Timothy would say from his bed. "You can do it" and do it she did. Annie received honors along with the English prize of $500.00 for her essay on Dr. Tom Dooley. She wrote the essay with a lot of help from Sister Catherine Joseph and when it was done she wondered if she deserved the prize. She spoke to Sister Catherine Joseph about her feelings.

"Did I deserve it?", she asked the kind nun.

"Of course you did, Annie. I just coached you and helped you with the research. You did all the work".

But Annie never did feel right about it.

After exams the talk was all about what to wear to the prom. Annie had decided on a rose peau de sois gown with short sleeves. Her parents had given her a beautiful strand of pearls as a grad gift and Kate had given her a mink shoulder wrap. The only thing that would make it perfect would be if Timothy could come to the prom with her.

Two weeks before the end of school Sister Catherine Joseph made an announcement to the class.

The Board has made a decision on who would be Class Valedictorian and they had chosen Annie Thompson. The room was very silent and they could hear Annie take a gasp. She stood up and said she was honored but couldn't accept because Janet deserved it, not her. Janet's marks were better and had been all through the school year. It wouldn't be fair.

The class was dismissed and Annie was taken to the office.

"How could you refuse?", Sister Catherine Joseph said in a raised voice. "I have worked with you and given my time to you and this is the thanks I get. Your father will be furious with you. Janet could never be Valedictorian. She is a Protestant. That would never be allowed". She paced the floor rolling up the long black sleeves of her habit and tucked her hands under the starched bib.

"Just because Janet is a Protestant is that reason enough to deny her what is rightfully hers? That makes no sense to me and my father has nothing to do with this. I don't deserve this, I didn't earn it. Janet did. Wait until everyone hears that because Janet is a Protestant she can't be Valedictorian. I was proud to be a graduate of St. Raphael's but now I'm not. This is disgusting. I'm going home". She picked up her school books and left.

The students were in their caps and gowns ready for the processional march into the auditorium. Annie looked around and spotted her parents, Kate and Joey. Timothy was not well enough to come. She would see him after the ceremony.

Diplomas were handed out and Annie received her prize for her English essay. Janet Lewis delivered the Valedictory address. When it was over Janet went to Annie and wanted to know why she refused to be Valedictorian.

"When we went to the office, Janet, Sister Catherine Joseph and a couple of members of the Board went over the marks again and realized they had made a mistake. Everyone knew you would be Valedictorian and you so deserve it. Where do you intend to go to university? Any plans?".

"No plans to continue with school, Annie", she said.

"Marcel and I plan to get married this summer and I hope you will attend our wedding".

Annie went to find her parents. She found them with Father O'Reilly and Father Sullivan.

"Well, congratulations, Annie", Father O'Reilly said.

"And now it is on to St. Mary's for you. It is a good school and you should do well there".

"I'm not going to St. Mary's. I've applied at the University of Toronto and if accepted that's where I'll be going".

"Don't be preposterous, Annie", her father said.

They all laughed except for Annie, Kate and Rose.

"I'll show them", thought Annie.

"Mom, I'd like to go home now and show Timothy my diploma. He will be anxious to see me and hear all the details. Let's go".

She burst through the door into Timothy's room throwing her cap and gown to the side.

"We're home Timothy and it was just a great afternoon.

Look at my diploma. I'm going to hang it in your room".

There was no response from Timothy. Annie went over and shook his thin shoulders and told him to wake up.

He took a tiny breath and said, "What's all the commotion about?". Annie stood there and wept.

Rose and Kate followed. Kate went to Timothy and while holding his hand discretely took his pulse. "This is not good", thought Kate. "How much pain is he in? Will we ever know? She had never heard him complain". She straightened out his weakened body, cranked up his bed and adjusted the pillow.

"Are you comfortable, Timothy?", she asked.

"Thanks, Kate", he said almost in a whisper. "I want to hear all about Annie's great day. What a fine looking diploma", he said.

Annie sat at the foot of the bed with tears still running down her face. She wanted to hug him and tell him how much she loved him, how she would never have made it without him by her side. But she sat there silently knowing now that the day would come when he would no longer be by her side.

"Why the tears, Annie. You should be dancing around with joy. You are now a graduate and will be off to university in a couple of months", Timothy said.

"I'm just happy that it is over with", she said.

"I just hope that I don't have to wait long for an acceptance letter from the university. Do you think it will take long, Timothy?. Do you think I'll get accepted?".

"Of course you will Annie. I have no doubt. Now why don't you go help Mom and Kate with the fancy luncheon they have prepared for you. And in a few hours you will be dressed and ready to go to your prom. What time is Mark picking you up?".

"He'll be here at seven o'clock sharp and I suggested to him that he bring me an orchid corsage. I don't want a corsage of carnations or roses. I want something different".

Timothy smiled. "You are definitely different, my Annie. One of a kind. Now I am a little tired. Run along while I rest and come wake me when lunch is ready".

Annie slid off the bed, kissed her brother and silently left his room.

CHAPTER 14

Three weeks later Annie stood in the front hall holding the letter from the University of Toronto. She walked slowly to Timothy's room, knocked and when he responded she opened the door and sat herself gently at the foot of his bed.

"It's here, Timothy. It's here. The letter from the university. I'm afraid to open it. What if I haven't been accepted? What will I do?".

"Open it, Annie. Open it now. I can't bear the suspense", he said with a smile. He never had a doubt she wouldn't be accepted.

Slowly she tore the envelope open and began to read.

She took a gasp, smiled, hugged her brother and said, "I'm in. I can't believe it. I'm in. I've got to go tell Mom".

Rose hugged and congratulated her daughter.

"It's wonderful, Annie. I'm so proud of you. What an accomplishment. There is lots for us to do. It says you have to be on campus in three weeks. Not a lot of time but we will have you ready to go", Rose said.

The night before Annie was to leave Timothy was rushed to the hospital. When Annie went into his hospital room she could barely see his face for the oxygen tent was around him. She gently reached under the tent and took his hand.

"I'm here Timothy and I'm not leaving until you wake up". She sat by his side for hours and he didn't move, he was barely breathing. Rose and Kate were there also. Finally Kate took Annie by the hand and said it was time to go. She could come back in the morning. Annie could barely move. She walked up to Timothy, with uncontrollabley tears, she herself could barely take a breath, and it felt like the lump in her throat was strangling her. She leaned against her mother and they walked out together. She turned at the door and saw Kate making adjustments on the equipment. Kate appeared to be so strong and in such control.

At home Rose put Annie to bed. When she fell asleep Rose left the house and for the first time drove to Acres Stables to find her husband and let him know their son would not make it through the night.

She had an idea where his stable was located. She drove around until she spotted his car. It was a very warm, quiet late summer evening. The frogs and crickets were singing their song as Rose stepped from her car. She didn't knock on the Tack Room door, just opened it and went in.

"John", it's Rose. Are you here?". There was no response. A clip board was from hanging from a nail to the right of the door. She took it down and looking for a blank piece of paper flipped through the racing schedule. She recognized John's handwriting but there was an unfamiliar script that she didn't recognize. It certainly wasn't John's, it was too feminine. She left him a note telling him that Timothy was in the hospital and he should meet her there.

Too worried about Timothy she gave no more thought to the strange handwriting. Returning to the hospital she found Kate sitting by Timothy's bedside. She got up when Rose entered the room, put her arm around her mother and said, "He's gone, Mom. He's gone. He never gained consciousness". They stood together and wept.

Rose sank into a chair. Her baby boy was gone. No parent should ever outlive their children. Life was so unfair. John never arrived.

Annie was in a half sleep when she heard her mother and sister open the door. She jumped out of bed, started getting dressed thinking they had come back to get her. She opened her bedroom door and saw her mother and she knew immediately that Timothy had died. Without saying a word she wrapped her arms around her mother and sobbed. The front door opened and her father walked in.

In a rage she flew at him, screaming that Timothy was dead and where was he. His horses and girlfriend were more important than his own son. She pounded her fists on her father's chest and before John could hold her she fell to the floor. Kate stepped in and soothingly picked her up and took her to her room. Rose stared at her husband. He walked toward her, his hand fell on her shoulder and she nodded quietly as he said, "Rose, I am so sorry". There was no acknowledgement on her part, yet her shoulder moved a bit when John said, "Will you be alright?".

The following morning Father O'Reilly arrived at the house just as Rose was leaving with Kate and Annie for Fitzpatrick's Funeral Home.

"Rose, I am so sorry. I know how you feel but he is better off. He is with his maker and at peace".

"Thank you", said Rose, "but you couldn't possibly know how I feel. Now please excuse me".

Rose, John and their two daughters drove to the funeral parlor. Mr. Fitzpatrick met them at the door. He was a quiet, regal man whose son, Mike, was a friend of Annie's. As Annie shook his hand she remembered how she and her friends would all laugh when they asked him, "how's business", and his reply would always be, "dead, very dead". Well, it was no laughing matter now and Annie felt guilt as she recalled the many times she heard his reply and thought it was funny.

They were escorted to the back of the room where caskets were lined up. Annie chose a shiny, mahogany one with satin lining. As she turned to her mother saying, "this is the one, Mom", Father O'Reilly stepped into the room. Annie went over to him and wanted to know why he was there, what did he want?". Before he could open his mouth she told him to get out.

John went to his friend, shook his hand, accepted his condolences and was assured that he would be officiating at the High Mass for Timothy.

"You will have to excuse Annie", John said. "It is obvious that she is very upset over her brother's death".

"I want him out of here", Annie screamed. "He's the one who wouldn't let Timothy be in the First Communion procession. "Don't you remember that, Dad. I do and here he is saying how sorry he is. The hell he's sorry".

Rose took Annie by the hand and lead her away as John and Father O'Reilly stepped outside.

"Annie, I want you to be strong. I need your strength to get me through this. Can I count on you? I need you to watch over Joey and we will get through this together", Rose said.

"I'm so sorry, Mom. I have only been thinking of myself and how much I'm going to miss him. I will do whatever you want me to do".

The funeral was scheduled for Saturday. It was a very black day. As they were leaving the phone rang. John answered.

"Yes, I will be there", he said. "The funeral will be over at three o'clock. That gives me a couple of hours to prepare for the race". He hung up the phone. Standing beside him was Annie.

"Do you plan on racing your horses tonight?", she asked in a very calm voice.

"Yes, I do", her father said.

"How could you? You are going to bury your son today and still race the horses? Are you crazy? Why would you do such a thing? Don't you care that your son is dead?.

He looked down at his daughter and never said a word.

It was the first time in years that Rose had been in a church. The Cathedral of the Holy Trinity with its stately ceilings that seemed to reach for the sky, the row upon row of votive candles all in their ruby red containers flickered. The organist was playing a solemn hymn, one that she had chosen. The pews were filled with friends, some of them crying, some of them stoic. She looked toward the altar and there was the casket holding her son. A spray of mixed flowers lay on top. As she stood with her family she started the long walk down the aisle. It could have been twenty steps or fifty, she only knew it was the longest walk she would ever take in her life.

After mass, the pallbearers carried the casket to the waiting hearse. Rose had chosen the pallbearers. Four of Timothy's friends, Tom Gallagher who Kate had accepted his marriage proposal and Mark, Annie's friend who spent a lot of time with Timothy. He had hurriedly come back from university for the funeral.

Holding her younger son's hand she stepped into the waiting car and the procession started for the grave site.

The hearse entered St. Joseph's Cemetary and winded around until it came to a stop. Still holding Joey's hand, her daughters supporting her on each side, her husband walking behind them, her shaking legs made it to the final resting place of her son.

After the funeral everyone went to the Shadow Inn for a late lunch. Having thanked each one for coming she asked John to take her home,

Reaching home she alighted from the car as John opened her door. She walked slowly up the walk, mounted the five steps to the front door trying hard not to steal a glance at the wheel chair ramp. Her keys were clutched tightly in her hand; they were damp from her perspiration as she inserted the key. She didn't move. John stood beside her and said, "Rose, I have to go to the stables. I won't be long". She wanted to shout, "Go, just go". His steps resounded on the walk. The purr of the motor and crunch of tires turning assured her she was alone. She twisted the key, pushed the door open. The stillness of the house engulfed her and her throat tightened. She felt the cool wood on her hand as she closed the door and walked into the living room. Rose did not glance around. Dropping her coat and purse on the chair she placed her keys on the desk. They made a metallic clang that startled her for the sound brought her thoughts to hearing a similar sound. What was it? Oh, God. One of the pallbearers' ring hitting the casket handle.

It was over. Her first born son dead at the young age of nineteen. Her world had stopped yet the world kept going around.

CHAPTER 15

Two weeks later Annie left for Toronto. The house seemed empty. It was just Rose and Joey at home. Kate's time was spent at the hospital doing her internship. Rose wandered through the house in a numb state. She must pull herself out of this deep depression and put all of her effort into Joey. He was such a good child and had been neglected by Rose. As hard as she had tried to spend time with him, it seemed Timothy claimed all of her.

Joey came home from school one rainy Friday clutching a small hockey trophy. He placed it on the hall table and went looking for his mother. He found her in the living room just staring into space. Crawling up on her knee he said, "it's going to be okay, Mom. I'm sad, too". Rose hugged her son and said, "let's go have a snack". As they passed by the hall desk Rose spotted the tiny trophy. Picking it up she asked, "what is this?". It's a trophy I won at our hockey game today. I got it for being the most improved player".

"This is wonderful, Joey. Your father will be so proud. He used to play hockey when he was your age. We should go see him now. I know he is at the stables for he called just before you came home".

They drove to the stables to find John. Rose parked the car and with Joey by her side she opened the Tack Room door. John was sitting on the leather couch with his arm around a woman. Rose recognized her immediately. It has been years since she had seen her this way.

"My God, Rose, what are you doing here?, he said.

"Your son Joey, you do remember you have another son, has won a hockey trophy and we came here to show you but it is very obvious you are occupied". She turned and left.

John arrived home fifteen minutes after Rose and Joey.

"We need to talk, Rose", he said.

Joey went upstairs to his room, holding his little trophy.

"I'm sorry, you had to find out about Theresa this way. After the incident when she hit Annie, it was shortly after she left the convent. She was the only one I could talk to and one thing lead to another. If you had been there for me this would never have happened", he said.

"Don't do a guilt transfer with me, John", Rose replied. "Where do we go from here?".

"Things can remain as they are, Rose. Nothing has to change".

"Don't be so naïve, John. Don't be so damn naïve. It would be best if you moved your things out and I will decide what I have to do", she said

Rose heard a car pull into the driveway. It was Kate with Tom Gallagher.

Opening the door to greet them, Kate put her arm around her mother and said she and Tom had decided on a date to be married, December first.

"That's wonderful", Rose said. "Your father is here, let's go tell him the good news". Joey came running down the stairs wanting to know 'what's going on'.

John didn't move out and for the next two months the house hummed with wedding plans. It was to be a small wedding, only close friends and relatives and they would then leave for a week in the Bahamas. Annie would be home for the wedding and would be Kate's only attendant.

The wedding day arrived and it seemed only yesterday that they were making plans. Where did the time go? Annie wore a short scarlet red velvet dress with a ring of red roses in her hair. The bride was stunning in a short white velvet dress carrying a cascade of white stargazer lilies.

As the guests filed through the receiving line they gushed with compliments to Rose and John. "What a perfect couple Kate and Tom were; how Annie had grown and how hard it was to believe that she was in law school, how tall Joey was becoming. The family stood there together unified but if the world only knew the truth. The perfect marriage. The perfect family. All of it a lie.

A month after the wedding Rose consulted a divorce lawyer. It was difficult to find a lawyer who didn't know John, perhaps they had heard of him because of his reputation but one that had never met him. The lawyers in town were a closely knit group. Rose had to be careful.

She met with Laura Parks who right off the bat asked her if she was having an affair.

"Of course not", Rose said indignantly, "but my husband is. I want to divorce him because of his affair".

Papers were filed and John was served.

Rose heard the slam of his car door and braced herself.

He came through the door, papers in hand, threw them in her face and demanded to know if she was in her right mind.

"I won't give you a divorce", he yelled. "You would have nothing if it wasn't for me. Look around, Rose. Do you want to give up your high standard of living? Do you want to keep Joey in a private school? Where are you going to get the money? You have nothing. Why you can't even get a bank loan, a mortgage, nothing without my signature. You just don't get it".

"I get the fact that you are having an affair with Theresa Williams. A former nun who taught your children, a woman who hit your daughter. A woman who thought she was teaching right from wrong to your children. How are you going to explain this to them, John. As a matter of fact how are you going to explain any of this to your friends and especially those at the church. John Thompson, a pillar of the Catholic church having an affair with his high school sweetheart. I felt for a long time that you were being unfaithful to me and the children. They say the wife is always the last to know but I knew I just didn't know with whom. When I went to see Father O'Reilly about a scholarship for Kate, I indicated to him that I knew what was going on. He assumed that I knew about Theresa, or is it Terry she goes by now and that is why Kate was granted her scholarship. The same scenario was played out when I went to him about Annie's scholarship. He thought I knew. Now you do what you want to do. As for me, I've made up my mind and there is nothing you can do to stop me. Your dirty little secret can remain a secret but on my terms".

"No. You'll not get away with this. This is my house. You leave and take nothing. Nothing is all that you will get". He stormed out of the house.

The next thing Rose felt she should do was tell her children before anyone got to them. Annie would be home for spring break in two weeks. Calling Kate, she asked her if she and Tom had time to see her that evening. Rose wasn't looking forward to it but her children had to be told. Joey was only eleven years old. Would he understand?

Arriving promptly at seven o'clock, Rose, Kate and Tom were together in the living room. Rose excused herself and went to get Joey.

"What's this all about, Mom", Kate said. "You have me worried, you are so serious".

"There is no soft way to give you this news. I am divorcing your father. This is a decision that I have made and it has nothing to do with you".

Kate did not seem visibly upset but Joey was very confused.

"Why do you want to divorce Dad, Mom?, he asked. "Don't you love him anymore. Doesn't he love us? What are we going to do? Do we have to move? Did I do something wrong? Is this my fault?".

"No, Joey, of course not. You have done nothing wrong. Your father loves you and will always be there for you. This is a something I have to do. You are not to worry about anything." Feeling assured he left and went to his room.

"When did all this take place, Mom? What does Dad have to say about it? I can't believe this. Why?"

"Your father has been having an affair for several years with a woman by the name of Terry or otherwise known as Sister Theresa. I have suspected for sometime that there was another woman but did nothing about it because I was so wrapped up in Timothy. Now that he is gone I don't have to put on a face for the world. It's like a white elephant sitting up in the living room. Everyone walks around ignoring it, hoping it will go away but it doesn't. I have to do this, Kate, as much as it is going to hurt it has to be done.

"Oh, my God. Sister Theresa. I would never have thought of her. She was so familiar but I couldn't put my finger on it. Now it all makes sense", Kate said thinking out loud.

"You knew your father was having an affair", Rose said, "and you didn't say anthing. You kept it to yourself. That must have been very difficult for you. What a burden to bare. Annie will be home in ten days and I will tell her. When you are talking to her please do not say anthing."

Rose was waiting for Annie at the air terminal. Her daughter came through the gate with a big smile on her face. She flew into her mother's arms and said how much she missed her and was glad to be home, even for a short while.

Annie kept up her chatter on the ride home telling Kate all the news, the friends she had made, how her grades were better than she ever expected and best of all she was part of a dance group, that Mark would be home for his spring break, too, and she really wanted to see Sister Catherine Joseph. They had kept in touch with letters and she was so encouraging to Annie.

"Life is good,", she said.

Annie would soon be nineteen years old; old enough to take the news of her parents divorce in a mature manner or so Rose hoped.

Rose made a cup of tea and she and her daughter were sitting at the kitchen table when Rose broke the news.

"Annie, I have something to tell you. This is very hard for me and I want you to understand. I am going to divorce your father".

Annie put down her teacup and looking straight at her mother said, "I'm not surprised, Mom. Being away from home I have done a lot of thinking. I've often wondered how you ever got through Timothy's funeral. It must have been so hard for you. Dad was there but he wasn't. It seemed he was always wanting to leave. He was around only when he had to be and with Timothy gone he's probably never around. He is never at home when I call. Do you suspect that he has a girlfriend, Mom?"

"He does have, Annie. He does have."

Rose knew what Annie's next question would be and should she tell her. She had never lied to her daughter before, why start now.

"Who is she, Mom?, Annie asked.

"Her name is Terry. Your father used to date her in high school. You would know her as Sister Theresa", came the reply.

"Sister Theresa. Sister Theresa", Annie said in wonder. "It was her. All those times I went to the stables and couldn't place that smell. It was her all along. In school she had a smell about her like perfume but I knew nuns didn't wear perfume. Guess I was wrong." Another white elephant.

That evening Annie went to see her trusted friend Sister Catherine Joseph.

"Only the family knows, Sister, that Mom is going to divorce Dad. He is having an affair with a woman by the name of Terry", Annie started. "She used to be a nun and taught me when I was going to St. Peter's. You know her. Her name was Sister Theresa", Annie said.

"Yes, I do know her Annie and I have known about the affair for a long time. I tried so hard to talk some sense into Terry but she wouldn't listen to her big sister. She wanted to leave the convent and be with John. It didn't matter who got hurt. I knew the divorce was just a matter of time after Timothy died. I am so sorry. I did what I could".

All Annie heard were the two words, big sister.

"Are you telling me that this Terry is your younger sister, your sibling. That all this time you were being so helpful to me, so encouraging it was all because of your guilt that your blood sister was sleeping with my father. You knew all the time. How could you look me in the eye knowing what you knew. You weren't a friend to me. You deceived me and I will never forgive you".

Tears were starting to well in Annie's eyes. I will not let her see me cry. Enough tears have been shed. She picked up her car keys and purse and with head held high walked out of the convent never to look back.

CHAPTER 16

Rose got her divorce and custody of Joey but little else. Her lawyer, Laura, laid out her rights and John was telling the truth. She had no rights.

'We've been lobbying for years to have the laws changed", she explained to Rose but it is a fierce battle

It seems we take one step ahead and two back. The men are in charge. John will let you stay in the house until Joey is of age. He will give you three hundred dollars a week for his support but he will not pay for Joey's private school. He will give no more money for Annie's living expenses. He is a man who can't believe that his wife would leave him. By putting all of these restrictions on you he honestly believes that you will take him back".

With the final decree in her hand, Rose left Laura's office. Joey would soon be out of school for summer vacation and Annie would be home. She would take one step at a time. She would have to get a job and that she did. She was hired at the Art Gallery. The gallery where she had worked when she was Annie's age. When Timothy was an infant. She would be paid fifty dollars a week. Her mother would watch Joey after school. It seemed she had come full circle.

Rose was very concerned about the money for Annie's education. How could she possibly manage on three hundred dollars a week. Even if Annie had a job there wouldn't be enough money. Funny, all the years she was married to John she never worried about money. She paid all the bills by checks that only John signed. He also gave her an allowance of fifty dollars a week, mad money he called it.

"We will get by, Mom. I will get a job and pay my own expenses and my grades will not go down. He will not win. I won't let it happen", said Annie to her mother as she was reading the want ads. "Here's a good one, Mom. The radio station is wanting a receptionist, its summer relief and they are paying $25.00 a week. I'm going to apply and I'll get it. Where's the adding machine? I'm going to figure out just how much money I can make this summer".

The following day Annie appeared at the radio station and filled out an application. The manager, passing by, stopped and asked her if she was Annie Thompson.

"Yes, I am", she replied.

"Well, I know your father very well. If you want this job, it's yours. You can start on Monday".

Annie didn't care that she got the job because of her father. She just wanted the job.

At the end of the summer Annie had saved one hundred and fifty dollars. She was very proud of herself when she handed the money to her mother.

"Annie, this is your money, you earned it", said Rose. You will be returning to school in a few days and you can use it. I'll be okay. Don't worry about me", her mother said.

It seemed like a short summer to Annie. There wasn't much time for socializing. Sister Catherine Joseph had called her several time, as well as Father O'Reilly. She never returned their calls. They were the past. She did manage to spend some time with Mark. He was doing really well in med school and talked to her about his future plans. He wanted Annie to be part of his future. Annie smiled and said that was a long way off. She had a law degree to get and that was her priority. Before Annie left for school Mark presented her with a friendship ring.

"It's just a friendship ring, Annie. No pressure", he laughingly said. Mark was leaving in two days.

She kissed him goodbye and promised to write and they would see each other at Christmas.

CHAPTER 17

Before Annie left for school Kate announced that she was pregnant. The twins would arrive sometime around Christmas. There was much celebrating. Rose was going to be a grandmother. Her heart swelled with pride. Annie danced around singing that she was going to be an aunt. Joey grabbed her hands and danced with her. Everyone stopped. It was the first time she had danced in the house since Timothy died and she was dancing with her little brother.

Kate had called her father earlier and said she wanted to see him. He was happy to hear from his elder daughter as there had been very little contact since he moved out of the family home.

"Would you like to come over here, Kate, say, around 8:00 pm", he said.

"Well, Dad couldn't you meet us at our place", was her reply.

"I could but Kate this is my life now. Your mother doesn't want me back and I don't want to go back. Too much time has passed for a reconciliation. My life is now with Terry and I am very happy. You have to accept that", he said.

Kate hesitated for a moment and then agreed to meet at his place.

"I'll give you the address and directions", he said.

"There is no need for that Dad, I already know where to go". How long ago had she followed her father to the

Cape Cod house and witnessed her father kissing a strange woman.

She was very nervous as she and Tom knocked on the door. The door was opened by her father but Terry was standing close by.

"Come in", he said. "It is so good to see you. It has been too long". Terry came forward. He put his arm around her waist.

"Hello, Kate", she said. Kate introduced her to Tom.

They went into the living room where tea was set. As Terry poured her hands were shaking so badly that Kate took over, passing the thin china cups to everyone.

"As happy as I am to see you, Kate, I'm very curious as to why you called? Many reasons have gone through my head but I can't come up with a logical one. Now set my mind at peace and tell me why you are here", her father said.

Kate looked over at her father. He seemed so at ease, relaxed and happy. He still was a handsome looking man with the infectious smile that she so adored. She loved her father.

"Well, Dad, we are here to tell you that you are going to be a grandfather of twins sometime around Christmas", she said.

John stood up, patted Tom on the back, hugged Kate and told them how happy he was.

"Your mother must be thrilled", he said. "By the way, how is she doing?"

Kate did not answer. After more pats on the back and congratulations, Kate and Tom left with the assurance that she would take care of herself, not work too hard and keep him posted on her progress.

The next day Annie was leaving for school. She didn't feel good about leaving. She felt her mother was much too thin and she didn't smile a whole lot. Annie believed that money was the problem and her mother was too proud to say. Well, what could she do to help? Very little. Maybe she could get a job in Toronto and send the money home.

She was livid with her father. Him with all his money and not giving Mom what she deserved. She hadn't seen him for almost a year and had no intention of ever crossing his path again. He could have his Terry and his two-faced friends at the church. How could they condone that relationship? They had their heads stuck in the sand. Why even Sister Catherine Joseph told her, when they met, that her father was just helping Terry out. She was his housekeeper.

CHAPTER 18

Arriving back in Toronto the first thing Annie did was buy the daily paper and searched out the help wanted ads.

The ad jumped out at her.

"WANTED: Dancers. Willing to pay up to $100.00 a show. Auditions to take place at the Chatelaine Club, 9002 Bloor Lane at 9:00 pm Saturday. Bring your dance attire".

"That's five days away", thought Annie. "I'll have time to practice. Thank goodness I signed up for jazz dancing, that may come in handy".

That Saturday night Annie borrowed her roommate's car and drove to the address in the ad. It was not in a very good section of the city but she found the club and stared up at the neon sign.

"WELCOME TO THE CHATELAINE CLUB - A GENTLEMAN'S CLUB"

A big man came over to her car and asked if she was here for the audition and if so to follow him. Annie picked up her dance bag, filled with her dance wear and followed this stranger into the club.

He led her to the back of the club and she found herself in a dressing room. There were eight other girls there for the audition.

"Take a seat", he said. "The boss will be here in a minute".

"Should we get changed into our costumes?", one of the girls asked.

"No, stay as you are. The boss will be here in a minute", he shouted.

The pretty redhead sitting next to Annie turned and asked her her name.

"I'm Annie Thompson", she said.

"Oh, God, girl, we don't use our real names in this business. What is your stage name? Mine is Paradise".

"Well, I don't have one".

"You better think of one before the boss gets here. I think you would make a good Orchid. Yea, tell him your stage name is Orchid". And Orchid she became.

Annie thought of Mark and the orchid corsage he gave her on prom night. Since then, on her birthday he always sent her orchids.

The boss strutted in wearing cowboy boots. His open shirt revealed six gold chains hanging from his neck. He glanced over at the nine girls and said, "okay", get into your costumes, make it snappy, I'll be back in fifteen minutes".

Eight girls scampered around, opening their bags, pulling out wigs, makeup, and stiletto heels. Annie sat there not knowing what to do. What she brought certainly wasn't what she needed. She got up to leave.

"Where are you going, Orchid? Hurry we only have fifteen minutes and he'll be back".

"I don't have anything", Annie said.

"Well, c'mon over here, between all of us we can find something for you. Hurry", said Paradise.

Fifteen minutes later Annie did not recognize herself in the mirror. She was wearing a long, curly blonde wig that itched her head; false eyelashes, blue glittery eyeshadow, a red beaded bra with matching short shorts and Paradise had tied a black lace wrap around her hips.

"You look great", Paradise said. "He's gonna love you, you have an innocent look about you. A baby face. You're gonna make a lot of money. You have great legs. Are you going to be able to dance in those stiletto heels? I'll bet you have never stripped before, have you?"

Annie admitted she hadn't.

"I'll show you the ropes. I've been stripping for five years and I've made a ton of money. This is a good club. The customers aren't allowed to touch you. God knows, they will try but the bouncers will take care of you. You just tip the bouncers ten dollars and you will be okay.

Fifteen minutes later on the dot the boss walked into the dressing room. He looked the girls over and led them to the stage. One by one the girls went on stage and did their routine. "It wasn't really dancing", Annie thought. "They just kind of walked around the stage, not even to the beat of the music, twirled around the brass pole and that was it". She could do this.

It was her turn to perform.

She stepped up onto the stage and as the music began she started to sway with the rhythm of the music. The lights were on her, the boss and the other girls were watching as she flowed from one end of the stage to the other. She was in her own world. The music stopped. Silence. Clapping hands started. She looked over at Paradise who was clapping the loudest and smiling up at Annie. The boss was even clapping.

"You're great", he said. "You're hired. The rest of you can go home. We have our new dancer".

"Oh, no", said Annie. "I can't stay if Paradise can't work here. We're a team and we dance together. I'm sorry but I can't work here without Paradise".

All the girls headed back to the dressing room.

"Alright, alright. She can stay, too. Oh, what the hell, all of you can stay. Yea, I know. The girls that dance together stay together".

Annie felt a little stab in heart as she recalled Bishop Fulton Sheen's words, "The family that prays together stays together".

"Be here Friday night at nine sharp. The doors open at ten o'clock and the guys will be lined up to get in. Be ready. There will be a Housemom here and she'll go over all the rules with you and I'm assuming you are all twenty-one". Annie said nothing.

Back in the Dressing Room all the girls gathered around Annie and thanked her. "We're here for you Orchid. Anything you want or need just let us know".

Paradise walked Annie out to her car.

"I'll see you Friday night, Orchid. Come a little early and I'll show you how to put on makeup. Don't go buying stuff. I'll get all the shit for you. You're gonna need some false eyelashes and false nails. I owe you one, my little friend, I owe you big time. I've been wanting to dance at this club for months. Had several auditions but never got lucky until tonight. She closed Annie's car door and disappeared into the night.

On the drive back to the dorm all Annie could think of was the money. Mom will never have to worry and she must never find out how I got the money.

CHAPTER 19

The following Friday Annie arrived at the club and looked around for Paradise.

"Are you the new girl, Orchid?", a voice said from behind.

"Yes", replied Annie. "This is my first night and I'm looking for Paradise".

"Paradise isn't here yet", the matronly woman said. "My name is Stella and I'm the Housemom. There are a few rules I have to go over with you before you start work. First and most important the customers are not allowed to touch you. We don't do lap dances here. You just stand in front of the guy and do your thing. This is just a topless club so only the top comes off. When dancing on stage you will do two numbers, one with your top on and the other with the top off. You will work four hours and get a hundred dollars cash after your shift. Any tips you get are yours to keep. You must tip the DJ, the bouncers and me. Tip whatever you want but the more you tip the more the guys will take care of you. Don't get involved with anyone who works here, it's the fastest way to lose your job. If it's a choice between a bouncer and a dancer, the dancer is always the one to go. Dancers are a dime a dozen. Any questions?".

Annie said, "no". It was after eight o'clock and no sign of Paradise. What in the world would she do, she brought nothing believing Paradise would keep her word. The clock was ticking away, eight-thirty and no Paradise. Annie broke out in a cold sweat as the dressing room door swung open and in flew Paradise.

"Orchid, Im so sorry I'm late. I stopped at the DJ booth and asked Harold about tonight's schedule. You will be the third dancer on stage tonight so that gives me time to get you ready. Come over here and let's get started. I'm so sorry I'm late, you must have been worried, I can tell by your eyes. Okay, let's start from the bottom up, here's a couple of G-strings, put one on".

She handed Annie a satin, royal blue strip of fabric which Annie felt left nothing to the imagination. She slipped it over her long legs and put on a matching pair of short shorts Paradise handed her. Next came a royal blue sequined bra.

"Come over here under these makeup lights. Sit down and close your eyes", Paradise said with a smile.

"You won't recognize yourself when I'm finished", she laughed.

She pinned up Annie's platinum curls and slipped a curly, short blonde wig on her head.

"I picked this wig for you Annie, because it has a jazzy look to it, it suits you", she said while adjusting the blonde curls.

Next came the pancake makeup, blue eyeshadow, pink rouge on her cheeks and pink lipstick.

"Okay, Orchid", she said. "I'm glad we wear the same size shoes. Try these on, they are my favorites, not quite as high as the other stilettos".

Annie slipped the silver stilettos on her feet. Stood up, looked in the mirror and gasped.

"Is that really me?", she said.

"You bet it is and you look smashing. Now practice walking around. You need to learn the stripper walk. Put a hand on your hip, as you take a step cross one foot over the other, hold your head high and smile. Now try it", Paradise said.

Annie did as she was told. She was like a duck to water. Sashaying across the floor, Paradise hollered, "you've got it Orchid, you've got it, swing those hips and smile".

Annie heard the DJ over the loud speaker in the dressing room.

"Our next beauty we have for you gentlemen is our newest gal, Orchid and here she is for your pleasure, how about a nice round of applause for her", he said.

Annie stared at Paradise.

"Oh my, it's my turn, can I do it, Paradise", she cried.

"You bet you can, now get going they are waiting for you. Hold your head high and smile, smile, smile. Go on, I have to get ready", Paradise said as she pushed Annie through the dressing room door toward the stage.

Annie climbed the few steps to center stage, grapped the brass pole and started her dance. The club was dark, just the lights were on Annie as she lifted her leg and wrapped it around the pole bending backwards. The men shouted and cheered.

"Take it off", they shouted, "take it off".

Annie looked down at the men sitting around the stage.

They were throwing dollar bills at her feet, she kicked them aside and smiled. Five dollar bills were being tossed now.

She continued dancing to the first song. The lights dimmed as her second dance started.

Paradise was watching from the corner.

"Take off your top, Annie, take off your top", she whispered to herself. But Annie didn't.

The men were now screaming, "take it off, take it off".

As the last bars of the song were being played Annie reached behind her, undid the bra hook, turned her back to the men and with the bra around her index finger, she twirled it in the air as the music ended and the lights went down. In a split second, Annie had the bra back on, the lights went up, she stood there smiling as the crowd roared.

Jeff, the bouncer was helping Annie pick up the money off the stage.

"I'll get this for you Orchid", he said. "You are beautiful and you sure pulled a fast one of these guys. They loved it. Paradise is up next, so get off the stage and I'll bring the cash to you".

As Annie left the stage Paradise took over.

Heading for the dressing room a customer grabbed Annie's wrist and asked for a private dance. Jeff was right behind Annie. With a smile on her face, she said, "I'll be right back".

Jeff followed Annie into the dressing room and they counted her stage money. There was a total of seventy-five dollars.

"Oh, yea", Jeff said. "They really like you".

Annie thanked him and slipped him twenty dollars.

"I'll watch over you like a hawk, Orchid, you're different. A lady. Not like the others. Anyone gives you trouble, I'll be right there to take care of the bastard". Now freshen up the lipstick, I'll be right outside, remember you have a customer waiting and he is a regular with a lot of money. You must have impressed him good because he rarely asks for a private dance".

"No, Jeff, wait for me. Please wait for me", Annie said.

Together they went back into the club, Jeff took Annie to her customer and stood a mere four feet from her.

The customer didn't want a private dance after all. He wanted to just sit and talk. He started by asking Annie a lot of questions about herself but Annie switched the conversation back to the him. She found out that he was married with three children, a surgeon at the General Hospital. He came to the club Friday nights only and hoped that Annie would be there next week. She assured him she would be. He got up to leave and handed her some folded money. Never once did he attempt to touch her.

Paradise was fixing her makeup as Annie entered the dressing room.

"How did you do, Orchid?", she said. "That guy you were talking with comes here every Friday. He's a big tipper".

Annie opened her hand and looked at the folded money.

"Count it, girl, count it", Paradise said laughing.

Annie counted five one hundred dollar bills. More money than she had ever held in her hands.

Annie started to tell Paradise how much money she had when Paradise stopped her.

"I don't want to know how much money you make. That's your business,. Don't tell anyone. There is a lot of competition here and they can make your life miserable. Go put your money in your locker, make sure it's locked up tight. If they can steal it from you, they will. Just take care of Jeff. He's a good bouncer and will look out for you".

"What do you do with your money?", Annie asked.

"You go to the bank and get a safety deposit box. That's the safest place for it", came the reply. "We just have another hour to work and then we're off. Do you want to get something to eat when we finish?"

Annie hesitated. She thought of the assignments she needed to have ready for Monday and she was very tired and as much as she liked Paradise she didn't want her to know anything about her. Best to remain club friends.

"I'll take a rain check, Paradise, if that's okay. I'm really tired and tomorrow I have to shop for new outfits. I can't thank you enough for what you have done for me".

"No problem", said Paradise. "Don't forget your tip for the Housemom. See you tomorrow".

The following night Orchid arrived with new outfits. She couldn't believe that she had spent one hundred and fifty dollars. That left her five hundred and five. She would go to the bank between classes on Monday and get that safety deposit box.

The following night when Orchid arrived at the club she was met by Jeff.

"The Doc is back, Orchid", he said, "and he is waiting for you. Get dressed quick. This is a first, he only comes in on Fridays. You must have really impressed him".

Annie dressed in a yellow sequined, short dress. She wore the short curly, blonde wig and gold stilettos. The false eyelashes with gold eyeshadow and a bit of gold glitter on her cheeks. Paradise clapped her approval.

Annie stepped up onto the stage and danced her routine. When it came time for her to take down the top of her dress, she coyly slipped the strap of her dress down as the song ended and the lights faded. Everyone applauded.

"It isn't what I came for", said one of the men, "but that girl sure has class".

The doctor was waiting as Annie came off stage.

"Come sit with me, Orchid. The manager said you could spend the rest of the night with me. I tipped him royally".

Annie laughed and said, "don't I have anything to say about this arrangement?".

As he took Annie's hand, she thought, "how many lives did his hands save this week? And what is he doing in a place like this when he has a family at home? Did it really matter. No. I'm here for the money only and if he wants to buy my company, then that is just part of the game".

That night the doctor left Annie and handed her folded bills. When she counted the money there was a thousand dollars. Jeff had picked up one hundred and fifty from her stage. She gave him fifty.

The Christmas season was approaching and Annie told the club she would not be available over the holidays. She would be on vacation for the month of December.

"You can't Orchid", the boss said. "We need you. Word is out that you're the best dancer, the best looking and the classest. You've got to be here. We'll be busy".

"Sorry, boss, but that is impossible", she said.

Final exams were just around the corner and Annie had a lot of catching up to do. She had worked very hard, burning the candle at both ends, but her education had priority.

There was plenty of money in the bank. In just the past two months of dancing she had stashed away close to eight thousand dollars, thanks to the doctor.

CHAPTER 20

Rose was waiting for her younger daughter who would be coming through the airline gate any minute. It had been three and a half long months since she had seen her. Too long a time for a mother not to see her daughter. There just wasn't enough money to have her visit and at the same time she also wondered how Annie came up with the money to come home for Christmas. The passengers were entering the air terminal and Rose strained her neck over the other people waiting to greet family and friends. She spotted her and smiled. As Annie came nearer Rose noticed a big change. Gone was her little girl and walking toward her was a very confident, beautiful young woman. She reached out her arms to enfold her daughter.

"You look wonderful, Annie", she said. "I have missed you so much. We have so much to catch up on".

Annie stood back and looked at her mother. Gone were the smiling eyes, the shine in her hair. She had lost a lot of weight.

"Mom, you look wonderful, too", Annie said. "How is everyone? Kate must be ready to have the twins and how is Joey making out in public school?

On the ride home Rose caught Annie up on all the news.

"We are expecting the twins any moment. They are a week overdue. Kate is getting more than a little anxious.

Joey is doing okay in school. It is a big change for him and he misses the friends he had at St. Michael's but he meets them every now and then and will spend time with them over the holidays. Christmas Eve your father would like you to go to his place for dinner and midnight mass. Kate, Tom and Joey will be there as well as some other people that you know. Christmas Day we will have dinner at the house".

Kate pulled up to the front door of her house and Joey came rushing out.

"Annie, I'm so glad you're home. It just isn't the same without you", he said as he grabbed Annie's bag and they headed for the house.

The house was decorated from floor to ceiling as Annie remembered from Christmases past. The seven foot tree was a mass of bubble lights, tinsel and perched at the top the Angel. There were presents under the tree.

Rose caught her eye and said, "Joey and I made the gifts and we hope everyone likes them. Kate and Tom are going to drop in later".

No sooner were those words spoken when the telephone rang.

"Rose, it's Tom and we are on our way to the hospital. Can you meet us there. Kate is in full labor. Dr. White is waiting for us at the hospital".

"We will be right there", said Rose.

"Hurry Annie and Joey. We are on our way to the hospital. I'm going to be a grandmother tonight".

The twins were born Christmas Eve morning. A girl and boy. Kate was glowing when Annie went in to see her.

"Fine job, Kate. The babies are perfect. You look radiant but exhausted. I'm so proud of you. Mom will be here in a minute, she can't drag herself away from the nursery.

"Have you decided on names for my niece and nephew?", she asked.

"We have decided to call our daughter Rosemarie Anne, after you and Mom and our son will be John Joseph after Dad and Joey".

Rose entered the room and went to Kate.

"They are perfect babies, Kate. How proud I am".

"Well, you are much too young to be a grandmother, Mom".

There was a quiet knock on the door and as it slowly opened John stood there holding a dozen yellow roses and two huge teddy bears.

"Come in, Dad. Have you seen the twins? Aren't they perfect?, Kate said.

John let go of the door and stepped in.

"Yes, they are perfect", he said.

He looked at Rose and said, "Congratulations, Grandma. It is hard to believe that we are grandparents".

He turned to Annie, went to hug her and she stepped back. Nothing was said.

A tension was building in the room and Rose said it was time to leave and let Kate get some rest. She would be needing it when she came home with the twins the next day.

It was a quiet Christmas Eve for Rose and Annie. After John picked up Joey for dinner, Annie put on a pot of tea and sat with her mother.

"Mom, how are you doing?. You don't seem very happy."

I'm fine, Annie, just a little tired. The art gallery was very busy during this season and I haven't had much time to myself. Things will settle down after Christmas".

"Have you done any painting? It has always been your passion and you are so good at it. I remember you painting my bedroom wall, freehand, all the characters from Bambie. You could start your own business. Think about it, Mom".

CHAPTER 21

All too soon Annie was back at school and back dancing.

"How was your Christmas", Paradise said as she walked across the dressing room toward Annie.

"It was good but it's good to be back", Annie replied.

Another New Year and Annie was calculating how much money she could put away over the next six months and keep her studies up.

"Hurry, Orchid", she heard Jeff call. "The doctor is in the house and asking for you. He has a present for you, hurry".

Annie put on the curly wig, the makeup and stilleto heels and donned a short green velvet strapless dress and headed for the club. There he was, the doctor, standing, waiting for Orchid.

"Happy New Year, Orchid. I have something for you. Let's go sit in the corner". He handed her a beautifully wrapped present and said, "open it".

Annie carefully slid the black velvet box from the wrapping. Brushed her hand across the soft fabric and opened it. A stunning emerald and diamond bracelet lay on a bed of satin. Annie took a deep breath and said, "it's beautiful".

"It's for you, Orchid, it will go well with the dress you're wearing tonight". He took the bracelet from the box and locked it on her wrist and took her hand. "It's a small token of how much I like spending time with you. Would you ever consider having dinner with me one evening? Away from the club? I would like to be your friend."

Annie didn't even know this man's name nor did she care to know. He didn't realize that dancing was her job and part of her job was to enertain customers. Not make friends with them. She wasn't here to make friends but to make money. She turned the bracelet around on her wrist.

"You haven't opened the card, Orchid", he said.

Annie slid the card from the envelope, opened it and there inside was two thousand dollars.

Her sky blue eyes looked at him. She smiled.

"Thank you", she said. "I will treasure this bracelet always".

"I can't stay tonight, Orchid. I am taking my wife to the opera and must leave now or I'll be late". He leaned over to kiss her on the cheek but Orchid was on her feet in a split second.

As Annie was putting the bracelet and money in her locker she thought, "what a rotten guy. He comes bearing gifts while his wife is waiting for him at home. He's nothing but a cheater. A cheater just like my father".

CHAPTER 22

Annie dialed her mother's number.

Rose answered. She could tell by her mother's voice that she had been crying.

"What's wrong, Mom. I can tell by your voice that you have been crying. Is everyone okay?".

"Yes, Annie, everyone is okay. The twins are going to be baptized this Sunday at the Cathedrale. I told Kate I would not be attending but hoped that she would bring the twins to me before the ceremony. She got very upset with me"

Annie hung up the phone and dialed the airline. She got a seat on an early flight the coming Saturday. She arrived unannounced at Kate and Tom's house.

Kate opened the door in utter amazement to see her sister standing in the rain.

"My God, Annie, is that really you. What are you doing here. Mom didn't say you were coming home. This is great. Perfect timing for the baptism tomorrow", she said.

"No, Mom doesn't know I'm home. I'm here to see you. Mom told me she won't be attending the baptism and you are pretty upset with her. You have no right. Mom was always there for you. You would never have gone to McGill and become a doctor if it hadn't been for Mom. Your place is to honor her wishes. If she doesn't want to go tomorrow, then that's how it is. Have you taken any notice of your mother? Have you seen how unhappy she is?". You're here in your snug house with the fires burning and Mom can barely make ends meet. Don't put any more pressure on her than she already has. The ball is in your court, Kate. I'm going to Mom's now and as far as she is concerned, we never had this conversation".

Annie ran through the rain to her rental car and headed for her mother's house. The house was very dark. Rain was still falling and the wind whistled through the trees.

Opening the door with her key, she called out for her mother. No reply. Annie walked through the house putting on all the lights. A fire was slowly dying in the fireplace, she stoked it, threw on a small log and got it roaring again. She went in search of her mother. She found her upstairs asleep on her bed. The tear stained pillow told Annie just how sad her mother was.

"Mom, it's me, Annie", she said as she gently shook her shoulder.

Rose sat up and without a word hugged her daughter and sobbed. She didn't ask how or why Annie got there. She was just glad she was.

The tea kettle whistled and Annie poured the steaming water into the teapot.

"Mom, tell me how I can make things right", said Annie. "You and Joey can't stay in this house any longer. It holds too many memories for you. You have to pull yourself together and live your life. It is not an easy thing for you to do but you can have a full life. You're still young and one never knows what's around the corner".

"I can't leave here, Annie. Where would I go? I also have Joey to think of. It seems that the friends your father and I had before the divorce have disappeared. People I knew for years. People I thought were friends. I'm so lonely."

"Mom, come to Toronto with me. We can get an apartment, there's a great private school Joey can attend. You can set up your easel and paint. You can do this, Mom."

Rose laughed at her young daughter. So full of life, of promise and hope.

"Oh, Annie, that would solve a lot of problems but there just isn't any money".

"Don't you worry, Mom. I'll think of something. I have to go back tomorrow after the baptism. You don't have to go. Kate will probably bring the twins here to see you and we'll take pictures. You, Joey and I will go out for lunch and have our own celebration. Don't you worry. I love you, Mom. Now let's go to bed and get some sleep we have a busy day ahead of us tomorrow".

CHAPTER 23

Annie boarded the flight back to Toronto and the stewardess asked if she would like the Toronto daily newspaper.

Opening the paper Annie turned to the want ads.

"Houses for Rent". Going down the many listings Annie saw the perfect ad.

"Three bedroom, two bathroom house for rent. Rosedale District, six hundred dollars a month, furnished, one year lease and the telephone number". This is a perfect location, thought Annie, on the streetcar line and she knew St. George's Boys School was in Rosedale.

The next day she went to see it. Dressed in her most conservative clothes, Annie rang the bell. A striking woman in her early thirties greeted Annie.

"Hello, Anne", she said. "I'm Loretta Robinson. Aren't you a little young to be renting a house on your own", she asked.

"Oh, I'm looking for my mother. She has been living out of town but will be here soon. When is the house available", said Annie.

"It will be available in six weeks. My husband has accepted a teaching position at the University in Montreal. We will be gone for a year. Come, I'll show you through".

It was full of color, bright sunshine coming through the beveled glass windows with a garden full of spring flowers. The solid oak staircase led to the bedrooms and at the end of the hall was a large sitting room that Annie knew would have the perfect lighting for her mother to paint.

Sitting in the parlor, Loretta Robinson went over the lease with Annie and asked for a deposit. Annie had six hundred dollars in cash. She signed the lease. Shaking hands with Mrs. Harrison, her heart very light Annie left and within a ten minute walk was shaking hands with the Head Master of St. George's Boys School, Mr. Armstrong". She knew by the glint in his eye that there would be no problem getting Joey into this school. She flashed her blue eyes and gave him her biggest smile. "Men were so transparent when it came to a pretty woman", she thought. "Like dogs in heat".

The only thing Annie needed now was a car. A car would save her a lot of time getting back and forth to school and a car would be needed when her mother and Joey arrived.

Six weeks later, after numerous phone calls and a lot of convincing Annie was driving to the train station in her new '65 yellow Mustang convertible to pick up her mother and little brother.

The wheels of the train came to a screeching halt with small sparks flying and steam rolling. She looked through the crowd but couldn't spot her mother. Walking quickly from one train car to the other, feeling that maybe they weren't on the train, Annie could feel the tears falling from her eyes. She was about to turn and drive home when she heard her name being called.

"Annie, Annie, over here. We're over here".

She turned and ran to her mother and grabbed her and little Joey in a hug.

"Thank God, you are here. I thought you didn't come", she cried.

"We're here and we have a lot of luggage. I'm sure Joey brought everything he owns. How will we ever manage to get all of our stuff together?" Rose said.

"Don't you worry about that, Mom. You and Joey wait here and I'll be right back".

Annie spotted a tall, good-looking man entering the train station. She went up to him and as he turned she realized he worked at the train station. He was holding his cap in his hand.

Looking up at him, she said, "Oh, could you please help me. I have the tickets to my luggage but can't seem to locate it". She smiled, blinked her blue eyes and handed him a twenty dollar bill.

"Well, lovely lady, it would be my pleasure to help you. My name is Andy. What's yours?"

Annie smiled again and said, "I think my luggage may be over here".

She led him towards her mother and within minutes two steamer trunks and eight pieces of luggage appeared. Annie looked in amazement. "I guess Joey did bring everything he owns", she laughed to herself.

"Mom, we'll just take the luggage that you will need when we get home. I'll make arrangements to have the rest delivered to the house".

The porter quickly jumped in and said, "Oh, I can bring it to you when I get off work. Just give me your address", he said.

"That won't be necessary", Annie said as she stepped inside the station and made the arrangements.

With three pieces of luggage stacked in the car, they left the station and headed for their new home and new life.

CHAPTER 24

The sun was brillant as Annie opened the tall, oak stained door and led her mother and Joey inside. The house was filled with fresh flowers, a bottle of wine was chilling and the cupboards and refrigerator were stacked with food.
Rose stood in the middle of the hallway, looked around this beautiful house and stared at her daughter.

"How, Annie, how did you do all this. How can we afford this. I have so little money", Rose said.

"Oh, Mom, we'll talk about that later. Now let's have a glass of wine and toast a new beginning".

As Annie poured the crisp Chardonnay, she lifted her wine glass to her mother and said, "To better days, and happy endings, Mom".

By this time Joey had gone through the whole house and found his bedroom. Rose and Annie heard him yell.

He came down the staircase holding a little, brown and white cocker spaniel puppy.

"Is he mine, Annie, is he really mine. The bow around his neck says, he's mine. Mom, hold him. Isn't he the best. I've always wanted a little dog".

Annie laughed and said, "yes Joey, he is all yours. Every boy should have a dog. Come I want to show you something upstairs".

They headed upstairs and into Joey's bedroom. Annie went to the window and said, "Do you see that tall building straight ahead, with the cross on top? Well, that is your new school. Their number one sport is hockey. The Headmaster, Mr. Armstong, is looking forward to meeting you. Mom and I will take you there on Monday".

They went downstairs.

"You and Mom can take the puppy out to the garden and think of a name for her while I prepare lunch", Annie said.

A half hour later Annie carried a tray of fresh fruit, salad and grilled salmon to the patio table. She poured herself and her mother another glass of wine.

"Lunch is served", she said.

After they had eaten and Joey was playing with the frisky puppy, he announced that he had the perfect name for her.

"I'm going to call her 'Spirit', he said. "Yes, Spirit is the perfect name".

It was getting close to eight o'clock and Annie knew she had to leave.

"Mom, I have to go out this evening. You must be exhausted and need a goodnight's sleep. We will talk in the morning."

Annie threw her dance bag in the back seat of her car and left for the club hoping that Paradise would be there.

"Paradise, are we allowed to leave our things in the locker or do we have to take everything when we leave?", Annie asked.

"Yea, we have to take everything home", came the reply.

The Housemom overhearing the conversation, pulled Annie aside and said, "I can give you a locker, Orchid. You won't have to take your things home every night".

"Thank you, Stella", Orchid said as she handed her a fifty dollar bill. "Amazing", thought Annie, "the power of the dollar".

That night Annie wore a white, toga style outfit with the short blonde wig and white stilleto heels. She wondered if the doctor would be in tonight. She hadn't seen him for several weeks.

Jeff came into the dressing room, told Annie how beautiful she looked and if she was ready, the doctor was waiting for her.

Together they walked into the club and Jeff took her to the doctor.

"I'm glad you're here Orchid", he said as he led her to the corner seats. As they sat together, he took her hand and said, "I won't be here for awhile. I have accepted a teaching post at the University in Montreal and will be gone for a year. I will try to fly down every month or so to see you but my schedule is very hectic. Here is my business card. If you should need anything, I beg you to call". He stood up to leave and handed her an envelope. He bent, kissed her on the forehead and left.

Annie opened the envelope and found five thousand dollars. She turned and found Jeff close by. He winked at her. She locked the money and business card in her locker and went back into the club.

"Over here, Orchid", Jeff said. "The Doc told me he wouldn't be back for a few weeks. Come with me I want to introduce you to a regular customer who has had his eye on you but knew you were off limits when the Doc was in the house. This guy used to be a top lawyer in the city but is now a Judge. He has money."

Annie was introduced to the Judge. A pompous, short, overweight, middle-aged man. He held an unlit, long, Cuban cigar between his fingers and leered at Annie.

"Well, aren't you a pretty one. I want you to get up on that stage and dance just for me and take it all off. Here's a hundred bucks. Now what do you think of that?", he said.

Annie snapped the money from his hand before he could make a move.

"That's a start", she said and walked away.

Paradise was smoking a cigarette, talking to a couple of other dancers when Annie went up to her and said, "Paradise can I borrow your red, long wig. I want to change my outfit too. What do you have that I can wear?".

"Why, what's going on. Of course you can have whatever you want", she said.

"Judge Anderson is out there and he wants me to dance for him. I don't intend to. What an arrogant, short, fat man. I would say he is a product of the small man syndrome". They all laughed.

Fifteen minutes later Annie went into the club wearing a red wig and hot pink mini skirt with a beaded bra. She walked up to the Judge, asked if he would like a dance and he said, "no, get lost, I'm, waiting for Orchid".

"You're going to have a long wait", thought Annie.

Annie locked up her dance gear, took the envelope and slipped it into her purse. Saying goodnight to everyone she headed for her car. Locking the doors, she snapped on the overhead light and read the business card.

Dr. Robert Robinson, Chief of Staff

Toronto General Hospital

CHAPTER 25

Over coffee and croissants the next morning, Rose asked, "Annie, how can we afford all this. Where is the money coming from to send Joey to a private school. I need some answers".

"I have a job dancing, Mom. I work Friday and Saturday nights at a club downtown. It pays very well and the important thing is that it hasn't interferred with my studies. I am still in the top five percent. I've been able to pay my living expenses since Dad stopped sending the checks, and also have paid for my schooling. Joey's school fees are paid until the end of the year. You have to trust me, Mom.

Now, when Joey is at school tomorrow I would like to take you shopping for new clothes and every artist's supply imaginable. I only have morning classes and we can have lunch at the Colonnade".

Weeks later Joey was excelling at school. Spirit would greet him at the door, yelping and jumping in circles. Rose had gained some weight and was showing again her passion for painting. Annie kept on dancing.

"Orchid", Jeff called. "There's a guy here who wants to meet you. I don't know much about him just that he owns an Art Gallery in Yorkville. Seems like a nice enough guy".

Annie dressed in her yellow outfit and went into the club.

"Hi, I'm Tony Matthews", he said to Annie shaking her hand.

"Hello, Tony", she said. "Let's go over here and sit down". The cocktail waitress put a champagne bucket and two glasses on the table. She popped the cork and poured the bubbly liquid.

"They tell me you're the best dancer here but you never take off your top completely. Why is that?", he asked.

"To me the dance is an art form.", she said.

He threw back his head and said, "art". "Funny you should say that because I own an Art Gallery".

For the next hour he talked about himself and his gallery. Annie listened very carefully and then said,

"Do you ever show new artists?".

"If their work is good, why do you ask?", he said.

"I have a friend who's work is very good. You should take a look at it. Maybe I could bring her to you?"

The thought of seeing Orchid outside the club appealed to him. "Maybe she would sit for me", he thought. It was arranged for her to bring her friend to the gallery the following Monday. The day when he viewed new artist's work.

"Gather up your favorite works of art, Mom", Annie said. "You are going to meet Mr. Tony Matthews owner of the Matthews Gallery on St. Clare Avenue. I'm sure he will love your work".

Annie pulled her long, blonde hair back in a ponytail, threw on blue jeans, a white blouse and hoped that he wouldn't recognize her.

"Are you ready, Mom?. We can drop Joey off at his hockey practice and head on down to the gallery", Annie said as she loaded the car with her mother's work.

A parking spot right in front of the gallery. What luck. Annie and Rose carried two paintings inside and looked around for Tony. He heard the tiny bell above the door ring and came to the front. After introductions, he inspected Rose's work. Annie wandered around his gallery and realized most of the art was of nude or semi-nude women. One in particular caught her attention. The model looked very familiar, posed in a dance position. This work was Tony's. She heard her mother and Tony approaching. They were shaking hands. As Annie left the gallery she breathed a sign of relief. He didn't recognize her. In fact, he barely paid her any attention, he was so intrigued with Rose's work.

Three months later Annie convinced Rose to open her own small gallery in the Forest Hill Village. Rose became known for her nursery rhymn character murals that she painted on the walls of children's bedrooms. The orders came flowing in and it was now a six month wait for her work.

Tony Matthews stopped in frequently. He finally got up the courage to ask Rose for a dinner date. She accepted.

CHAPTER 26

A new school year was beginning for Annie, her last and Joey now had just two years of high school. She often wondered where the time went.

She came home to an empty house on a late autumn afternoon. Spirit was there but only interested in Joey's footsteps. She walked slowly back to her wicker bed with head hung low.

The phone was ringing.

"Hello, Annie Thompson speaking".

"Annie, it's Kate. How are you? It has been a long time since I've seen you and I would like to come for a visit and bring the twins".

"We would love to see you. When can you come? The sooner the better. Mom will be so happy", Annie gushed.

The following weekend Annie was at the airport picking up Kate and the twins. It was a very happy reunion. The twins were now two years old and full of energy. Poor Spirit hid for their entire visit.

Sitting in the garden enjoying a glass of wine Annie realized it had been years since the three of them had sat down at the same table.

Rose asked about John and before Kate could reply Annie jumped in and said, "There is no need to hear about him".

"He was my husband for seventeen years, Annie. He is your father and grandfather to the twins. Of course, I'm interested in knowing how he is doing."

Kate told them that John was not well. He had been diagnosed with a terminal disease but was getting treatment and they were hoping for the best but prognosis was not very good. He was in and out of the hospital and Terry was taking care of him when he was at home. He still managed the law firm but didn't spend a lot of time at the office. He had sold his horses a few months back because of his health.

Annie had flashbacks of Acres Stables and the Tack Rom. "How could Mom care about a man who hurt her so much, who ran his horses the day his son was buried. Who was living with a woman who broke all her vows to the church. She may have forgiven him but Annie never would".

Annie spoke up and asked, "When is he going to make an honest woman out of Terry? Doesn't he think it is time that they got married?".

"Annie, don't be ridiculous", Kate said. "You know they can't marry, Dad's divorced and besides Terry is just his housekeeper".

Annie laughed. "You are in such denial, Kate", she said. "You believe everything that man says".

The conversation was interrupted by the ringing of the telephone.

"I'll get it", said Rose. "I'm expecting a call from Tony. He would like to come over and meet my daughters".

But it wasn't Tony. It was Mrs. Cohen, Mark's mother.

"Kate", she said. "Is Annie there with you?".

"Yes, Rebecca, she is. Why? Is anything wrong?".

"Mark has been in a terrible accident. He was traveling home from University and was hit by a drunk driver. It isn't good and we don't know if he is going to make it. I thought Annie would want to know. They were such good friends in high school and have kept up a correspondence for the past few years."

Kate broke the sad news to Annie.

"I'll leave in the morning", she said. It was decided that Kate and the twins would leave with her.

Annie entered Mark's hospital room. His private nurse was sitting in the corner holding his chart. She walked slowly to Mark's bedside. His head was bound in sterile bandages with bright red blood stains seeping through, his closed eyes circled in black. The only sound was the bleep of the heart monitor. She took his hand in hers and spoke his name. A faint squeeze. She remembered how they had walked hand in hand at the Pavilion. He was her friend. A friendship born out of kindness and respect and eventually love. Through their numerous letters and telephone calls they had dreamt of a future together. The bleep of the monitor became a long steady hum. Reality stared her in the face. She was numb, could feel nothing, not even the hot tears flowing down her face onto the starched white collar of her blouse. A small moan escaped from the knot in her throat. Her heart ached in the breathing silence. The pain locked her heart.

CHAPTER 27

The lease on the Harrison's house would soon be up and Annie had to make some decisions. There was three months left on the lease and two months until her graduation from Law School.

Over dinner Annie approached the subject of purchasing a house with her mother.

"But Annie", Rose said, "I never thought my move was going to be a permanent one".

"Why wouldn't it be, Mom", replied Annie. "Joey is doing so well at his school, involved with his hockey; your art work is selling, what is there to go back to? Dad has moved on with his life, he is set up in his own world with Terry. It's time to let the past go and live your own life".

Annie was right. Joey was thrilled to know that they would be staying and was excited to start house hunting.

"What about the money, Annie. Where are we ever going to get enough to purchase a house? Kate said.

"That shouldn't be a problem, Mom. The Gallery is doing really well. We just have to find someone to give us a loan", Annie said.

It had been several weeks since Annie had danced at the club and she was looking forward to seeing everyone this Friday night. Parking her Mustang, Jeff came running over to her car.

"Where have you been, Orchid? We sure have missed you the past few weeks. The Doc was in looking for you as well as Tony, the art fellow.

"It's good to be back, Jeff. How is everyone? Annie said.

Entering the Dressing Room, Paradise and the other girls hugged and welcomed her back. No one asked where she had been, it was no one's business.

Paradise brought her up to date on the club. Nothing had changed. But everything had, thought Annie.

"Are you just about ready, Orchid? The Doc is here waiting for you", said Jeff.

Annie gave a little smile and said, "Tell him I'm worth waiting for". Everyone laughed.

Dr. Robinson was elated to see Annie.

"You look wonderful, Orchid", he said. "It has been such a long time since I've seen you. I've ordered champagne for us. Come over here and let's get caught up".

Annie gave her biggest smile and let him lead her over to the table.

"I have great news", he said. "I will be returning home in three months and I hope you will really think seriously about having dinner with me. I've thought so much about you, Orchid. When I come back I'd like to set you up in a house, take care of you. You could go to school, be whatever you want. This is no place for someone like you".

"I'm just trying to get ahead. I take care of my little brother and mother and I want to get a house for us.

I have a little saved for a down payment', she tearfully said, playing him for all she could. "But I don't know if I could ever get a loan".

"That's easy, Orchid. I'll give you the name of a real estate broker and he will help you. This is his number call him tomorrow. He will definitely work with you".

He poured them a glass of champagne thrilled that he could help his beautiful Orchid. "Dance for me, Orchid", he said. Annie did and was rewarded with a thousand dollars.

The following Monday, after class, Annie met with the broker. She made no mention of Dr. Robinson. After viewing several homes with her mother, they decided on a four bedroom Tudor style, close enough to Joey's school and Rose's shop. The seller, a man in his fifties, couldn't take his eyes off Annie and when the papers were signed he asked Annie to dinner. She smiled, batted her blue eyes and thought, "Men are so easy to read. They see a pretty girl; think there is something in it for them. Their brain shuts down and every thought goes south of the belt". He had served his purpose, Annie got what she wanted. There would be no dinner.

CHAPTER 28

The Chancellor of the University was announcing her name. Annie walked across the stage of the McGregor Hall and accepted her law degree. Kate had arrived the day before. It was wonderful to see her. They celebrated by going to the finest restaurant in the city. Over dinner Kate handed Annie a letter from her father congratulating her and a check was enclosed. Annie said nothing. Just handed the check to her mother and said, "This is only a tiny bit of what that man owes you".

In two weeks she would start articling at the Cooper and Tucker Law firm at the bottom of the totem pole. Pay her dues and write the bar exams. She would dance for the next two weeks.

"Mom, I'm going to be working a lot over the next two weeks", Annie announced. "The dance theater is going into rehearsals for a new musical production. Between the money I'll make with all this extra work and what the gallery is bringing in, we'll be able to furnish our new home in style".

"Tell me more about your theater group, Annie", Rose said. "I know so little about where you work and I would like to attend one of the performances. It's been a long time since I've seen you dance".

At that moment Joey arrived home from school. Spirit was at his feet wagging her tail. They heard all about his day and Annie's dancing was forgotten.

Monday night Annie pulled into Club Chatelaine to the surprise of everyone.

"I'd like to dance four nights a week for the next two weeks", she explained to the Manager. "Will that be okay?"

"You can dance any night of the week that you want, Orchid", she was told. "It is always good for business when you are here. As a matter of fact, Tony the Art fellow is here and he will be very surprised to know you're dancing tonight".

Annie changed into her costume, donned the stilettos and went out to meet Tony.

After a lot of small talk, they sat down and he proceeded to tell her about the wonderful woman he had met and was dating. "Her name is Rose and she owns an Art Gallery. Her work is fantastic, just paints murals of storybook characters. I'm very serious about this woman, Orchid. That doesn't mean that I won't be coming to see you every now and then, it just won't be as often. She has two kids. One of them just graduated with a law degree and her son attends St. George's. I'm having dinner with her tomorrow night".

Tony stayed another hour but before he left he handed Annie two hundred dollars. "I'll be back", he said.

The following day Annie suggested that they all go out for dinner.

"Oh, I would like that, Annie", Rose said, "but I have plans to have dinner with Tony tonight".

"Have you been seeing a lot of him, Mom?" Annie asked. "You haven't mentioned anything to me".

"I have seen him quite a bit. We've had dinner and been to the theater and he has been an incredible help at my Gallery. I really like him. He is a good friend. He would like to meet you and Joey but I'd like to get to know him better.

"Be careful, Mom. You were married to Dad for a long time and things have changed since you dated. Your Gallery is doing fine. You don't need a man's help. You're doing fine on your own", Annie said.

"What about you Annie?" Rose asked. "You're young and beautiful. It seems you spend all your time working. Isn't there a young man in your life? You never talk about what's going on in your life".

"I don't have time, Mom. They're all the same. Men. You give your heart and soul to them and they just leave you in the end. When Timothy died he took a part of my heart with him. And then there's Dad. A man I trusted, looked up to and he betrayed all of us. Mark. The one person that I gave myself to. We had such plans for the future and he's gone. It won't happen, Mom. I'll never trust another man.

Somewhere between understanding and forgiveness there is a wall too wide for me to get around". Annie brushed the hair back from her eyes and her mother saw tears.

CHAPTER 29

Annie stepped into the revolving door of the Cooper & Tucker building. It moved slowly as she pushed on the high glass door. Stepping out Annie's heels clicked across the marble foyer as she made her way to the bank of gleaming, brass elevators. A group of five young men and two women were waiting for the elevator car to arrive. Two of the men glanced her way and gave her a big smile. Annie didn't respond. She glanced up at the floor indicator needle as the elevator made its way down from the 10th floor. The door opened and the men stepped in followed by the women.

"Typical", thought Annie. As Annie stood with her back to the men she could feel their eyes on her and the questions they were asking themselves. The elevator stopped on the fifth floor and the men all moved at once to get out brushing up against the women. The last man to exit brushed his hand across Annie's backside. As he did Annie grabbed his wrist. He turned with a very surprised look on his face but with no apology. One thing Annie learned at the Club was how to fend off roaming hands.

As the door closed the two women were smiling.

"That was a pretty fast move you made", one of them said.

"Hi. I'm Marilyn and this is Beverly. You must be new here".

"Yes", Annie replied. "I'm Annie Thompson and this is my first day".

"We work in the steno pool and if we can help you with anything just let us know. Where will you be working?" Beverly said.

"I'm here to article for the next ten months", said Annie.

"Oh, guess that means we won't be seeing a lot of you. The lawyers don't socialize with us. We're just the drones", came the reply.

The elevator doors opened on the seventh floor and the girls got off, wishing Annie good luck. Three more floors up and Annie was introducing herself to the receptionist. There wasn't one thing on her desk except a black telephone with four lights flashing. She picked up the phone, pressed a button and announced Annie's arrival to a voice on the other end.

"Mr. Cooper will be right with you", she said.

Ten minutes later the tall double mahogany doors opened and Mr. Cooper, senior partner, stepped into the reception area. Annie had met him during her interview.

"Well, welcome to the firm", he said. "Come this way with me and you can meet the other two students".

Annie followed him through the mahogany doors into the main office. He led her through a maze of tiny offices which ended in a small meeting room where the other students were waiting. After introductions they were paraded through the facilities and taken to the area where they would spend the next ten months.

"Are you working late again tonight?" Rose asked her daughter. "It seems we never see you anymore and we miss you".

"Yes, it's work again tonight, Mom. These sixty hour work weeks are getting me down. But it won't be for much longer. Two more months and I'll be finished and then more study for the bar exams. The firm has offered to pay for my bar exam and will keep me on salary, such as it is, while I'm studying. They also have indicated that there would be a position for me on passing the exam. It seems all I've done is spend time doing research while being rotated from department to department. I'll be glad when it is all over".

Annie thought of how unfriendly a place it was. There was no time for idle chatter or socializing. Several of the lawyers had asked her out to dinner but her stony refusal soon sent them running. They had nicknamed her "Ice". Annie laughed to herself when she heard that. Ice was a dancer at the club. Her thoughts wandered back to the club as they so often did. She missed Paradise and the camaraderie of the other girls. Maybe she would go there this Saturday night. She had been working weekends at the firm but this weekend would be hers.

She rang the back dressing room door and was buzzed in by the Housemom. She heard her holler across the room, "Guess who's here, girls. It's Orchid".

As Annie opened the door she was met and hugged by ten girls. The questions went flying. "Where have you been? We were worried about you. Are you back to dance or just visiting?"

She heard Paradise's voice, "give the girl some space, you're suffocating her". The other girls stepped back and Paradise hugged Orchid.

"It's good to see you, girl. I think about you all the time and keep waiting for you to come through that door and here you are. Are you working tonight?"

"Yes. I'm here to work and it is really good to be back".

"Well, hurry and get ready. There is a big bachelor's party going on. Lots of lawyers with lots of money".

Annie went to her locker and took out a lavender short dress. She sat side by side with Paradise putting on her makeup and felt at home. There was no pretense here, no one looking over your shoulder waiting and hoping for you to make a mistake. It was a safe feeling.

"Orchid, I heard you were here. Where did you park? I didn't see you coming in?" Jeff shouted as he hugged her.

"You have certainly been missed particularly by a certain Doctor who is in here on a regular basis looking for you. He gave me his phone number to pass onto you. I know it's against the rules but he insisted".

He took from his pocket a tattered piece of paper with Dr. Robinson's number. "How long had he been carrying it around?" thought Annie.

"Let's go, Orchid. The men are waiting", said Paradise.

They left the dressing room together and as Annie passed by the trash can she threw the ragged piece of paper in the garbage.

The club was packed and noisy. Paradise led Orchid to the bachelor party. Annie worked the group with her eyes and was amazed to find the elite from Cooper & Tucker smoking cigars, downing straight Crown and in general making absolute fools of themselves.

One of them grabbed Annie by the arm and demanded a dance. She glared down at him. He took out his wallet and extracted a twenty dollar bill. Annie started to move away. He pulled her down on his lap and told her she was nothing but a stripper and she was probably not even worth twenty dollars. In that split second Jeff and Paradise pulled Annie off the man's lap. With his brute strength Jeff picked up the man and threw him out the door. The other men in the group took no notice and continued to party. A familiar voice leaned over and said, "Where have you been?".

Annie turned and Dr. Robinson was there. He took her over to their regular table and ordered champagne. For the next hour he told her how much he had thought of her and how happy he was to see her. Annie turned on her biggest smile but kept glancing over at the bachelor party. Most partners were there including Mr. Cooper.

"Do you know those men, Orchid?", he asked. "You keep looking over there. I know who they are. They are all members of the law firm that I deal with. Cooper & Tucker.

One of the partners is getting married next Saturday.

Orchid didn't reply. Just smiled and changed the subject.

CHAPTER 30

Finally, the articling phase of Annie's career was over. Now it was time to study for the Bar exams.

"Are you all prepared for the exams?", Mr. Cooper asked Annie as he sat down in a chair next to her desk.

"I am very confident that I will pass", said Annie.

"Well, you know the firm will pay for you to take the exams."

"I appreciate your offer but I have already taken care of that expense", said Annie.

"Well, have you given any thought to our other offer of coming on board with us?", he asked.

"I haven't been given an offer", said Annie.

"Well, perhaps we could talk about it over dinner. I've watched you very closely over the past months and you are quite unique. I'd like to get to know you better, so what do you say about dinner?', he asked

"Sorry, but I don't mix business and pleasure. When I pass the Bar I will consider any proposal you may present to me", she said.

As he got up to leave, he leaned over resting his hand on her shoulder and whispered, "You'll change your mind about dinner".

Arriving home late, Annie found her mother and Joey in the living room going over brochures from various universities.

"What's going on?", she asked.

"Well, Annie, I just have another year of school and have to decide what I want to do when I graduate", Joey said.

"Gosh, it doesn't seem possible. The time has gone by so quickly. I remember when I was applying, Joey, it is a process, a tedious one, but worth the time. What schools are you considering and what do you want to study?", she asked.

"I want to study medicine at the University of Montreal. It isn't very far from Toronto. I could get home to see you and Mom but it is difficult to get accepted and it's expensive", he said.

"You'll get in. If this is what you really want, don't take no for an answer. Your marks are excellent and I'm sure Mr. Armstrong will write a superb letter of recommendation. Don't worry about the money, Joey. I'll take a position at the law firm. I know they are going to give me a proposal. Between my job and Mom's Art Gallery, we'll make it"

Rose sat quietly watching and listening to her daughter. "How did this come to pass", she thought. Annie had been organizing their lives for the past several years, daring anyone to say no to her. Fortunately, she had been right in all of her decisions especially in convincing her to move to Toronto. She had missed home, particularly Kate and the twins. The few visits she had back home were always so brief and left her a little sad when she had to leave. She had given up the hope that the past could be different. Given up the hope that John would come after her and want her back. Accepted her present and looked forward to the future and wondered what the future held for Annie. Annie. The apple of her father's eye who she refused to acknowledge. The first man in her little girl's life. The one man who would protect her, love her unconditionally, instill trust and security in her, he had let her down. His wants and needs were more important than hers. The pillar of the Catholic Church, the perfect family man had left his family for his lover, a former nun. Funny, how quickly the congregation forgave him and how quickly former friends turned their backs on Rose, whispering, "It was probably her fault", shunning her but welcoming the traitor. Despite the past Rose felt her present life was satisfactory. Her art was selling very well and she had Joey and Annie. Her thoughts were interrupted by Spirit's barking at the door bell. She picked up the dog as she opened the door. A delivery of flowers for her. She signed for the long, silver box tied with dark blue ribbons and reached behind her for the jar of lose change and bills on the hall table. She tipped the delivery man and closed the door. Spirit's barking brought Joey and Annie into the living-room as Rose was opening the box of beautiful long-stemmed roses.

"Who sent those magnificent roses?", Annie asked.

Rose opened the card.

It read: "Will you have dinner with me? Please call".

They were from Tony.

Rose was blushing.

"Who is he, Mom?", Joey asked. "Are you going on a date with this guy?"

"He is a person who helped me when I was opening the gallery. I haven't seen him for quite awhile and yes, maybe I will call him and have dinner", Rose said smiling.

She looked up at Annie. Annie was smiling. She saw her mother's eyes light up as she read the card and realized she had missed him.

Tony was very excited to hear from Rose. The following evening he took her to a very small, intimate French restaurant, The Bouquet, in Yorkville. There were only twenty tables, all occupied with couples. The owner's wife, dressed in black and white, her hair pulled tightly back in a bun wearing no makeup, smiled and presented them with heavy leather menus. She reminded Rose of the nuns at the convent. He ordered a fine bottle of Chardonnay and their dinner order was taken. Rose was amazed at the art work on the walls, the restaurant was lit with candles. It was clear this restaurant was for couples only. Tony reached across the table and took Rose's hand.

"I have been thinking so much about you, Rose and have missed you", he said.

Rose looked across the table at Tony. He was a very good looking man. Tall with a fair complexion. Jet black hair, blue eyes with lashes as thick of brushes. When he smiled deep dimples appeared. Rose admired the way he dressed. He could have been a model he wore clothes so well. As she smiled at him she realized she had been missing his company. Missed their conversations about art.

During the time Rose had known Tony, he told her he spent some of his time at a gentleman's club and most of his drawings were of the dancers. It started with him just sketching the girls at the club but soon one by one they came to his studio and that is how his collection of "Dancing Girls" started. The paintings were greatly received by his clientele. He offered to pay the girls for each sitting but they refused the money. They told him they made plenty of money. So, he would go to the club and talk with the girls and pay them for their time. A lot of these girls are well educated and know a lot about art. As a matter of fact, one of the dancers had told him of an artist that she was sure he would be interested in but she never came to the gallery.

"Was that recent?", asked Rose

"Well, it was some time ago, right around the time I first met you", he said.

"Where is this club?, asked Rose.

"Not too far from here", he said. He continued, laughing, "Why, Rose, would you like to go to the club, you would be like a fish out of water. I'll drive by on our way home".

Ending the dinner with a cognac, Rose was ready to go. She really enjoyed the evening with Tony but desperately wanted to drive by the club.

The massive, brightly lit sign of the club Rose could see a block away. As they approached Tony slowed down.

"Would you like to go in for a night cap?", he asked. Rose looked across the parking lot and her heart stopped; it was Annie's yellow Mustang. Annie had been dancing in a strip club to pay for her education, moving her and Joey to Toronto, buying the house and now taking care of Joey's education.

Tony looked over at Rose and said, "Are you okay, Rose, you look as though you have just seen a ghost".

CHAPTER 31

Over coffee the following morning, Rose looked across the table at Annie and asked, "Where were you last night?".

Surprised, Annie said, "Why do you ask?".

"Don't play word games with me, Annie. Tony and I drove by the Chatelaine Club last night and I saw your car parked outside. I know it was your car because we were close enough that I could see the license plate. What were you doing there?", Rose asked.

"I was working, Mother, I was working", Annie answered defiantly.

"So you've been dancing at a so called gentleman's club. How could you, Annie. How could you. I thought I taught you better. How could you do such a thing?. This is totally unacceptable. My God, what would your father think. He isn't well and finding this out would surely break his heart".

"It wouldn't matter to me if he does find out. Who is he to be telling me what to do with my life. He's the one who walked out on us. Left you high and dry. Betrayed all of us with his lies and false promises. He is a hypocrit. Still going to mass and receiving communion. His old buddies at the rectory covering for him. John Thompson, successful lawyer, an adulterer. He would be a fine one to ever judge me.

I dance at the club for the money, Mom. It was a conscious choice. I needed a job that would pay lots of money but wouldn't interfer with my studies. When I saw the ad in the paper I didn't know it was a strip club but when I went and found out just how much money could be made, I made my decision. It isn't that much different from ballet, Mom.

All dance is a form of art. When I put on my first pair of stilettos I thought of them as wearing my hard toe slippers with training wheels. My costumes are made of silk, satin, velvet and chiffon. The same fabrics I wore as a ballerina. The only difference is when I perform on the club's stage, the men who sit around the stage throw money, lots of money. Men who you would never dream would go into such a club. Married men more faithful to their regular dancer than they are to their wives. Single, professional guys living a fantasy that will never be realized and all the while handing over hundreds of dollars. Stripping. I call it the art of the tease. I tease, lower and bat my eyes with unspoken promises that will never happen. I'm in control and I get what I want".

"You don't have to go there anymore, Annie. We have enough money. You are doing well at the law firm and my gallery has grown beyond my dreams. There is no need to continue. You can't go back", her mother said tearfully. "Promise me you won't go back".

CHAPTER 32

Annie grabbed her car keys hurrying out the door. A tough case to litigate in court today. Did she have a good defense? Getting to the office an hour early would insure that the file was complete. Traffic was light at five am. She slipped in a tape of her first case to start at nine o'clock. She couldn't forget the slightest detail. She learned a long time ago, "it didn't matter who was right or wrong, innocent or guilty, it was a game and the winner took all". She hoped it wouldn't take too long. She had to meet her mother and Tony at Convocation Hall for Joey's graduation at four o'clock. Another doctor in the family. He would be a good doctor. "He is such a strong man", Annie thought, smiling to herself as she remembered his growing up in a house with two single women. Kate was to be here but couldn't make it as Dad was back in the hospital again and she was needed there.

Unlocking the door to her corner office on the thirty-fifth floor, she turned on the lights. The shrill sound of her phone ringing startled her. "Who could be calling me at this time of day?", she thought. She reached for the phone.

"Anne Thompson speaking", she said.

"Oh, Annie, I'm so glad you answered", Kate cried into the phone. I tried calling you at home but there was no answer. Dad died an hour ago".

Seconds that seemed like hours passed.

"Annie, are you there, please say something".

Anne took a deep breath, "What do you expect of me, Kate?".

"I expect you to come home. I need you", she said.

Years flashed through Anne's mind. How long had it been since she was home? Ten, maybe fifteen years? Kate was talking but Anne didn't hear.

Kate, always the peacekeeper, the one who danced around the invisible elephant that was forever present in their home, needed her.

"Annie, please come", she almost begged. If not for him, Annie, come for me".

CHAPTER 33

What a miserable day. The cold rain was falling in sheets. The bang, bang of the windshield wipers was mesmerizing. This city was so depressing, how she hated coming back.

She pulled up to the solid brick home and the front door opened. Tom, her brother-in-law rushed out to get her bag. "Thanks for coming, Annie. I know this is not easy for you".

Entering the house, the two sisters hugged, one sobbing; the other had a hard look on her face as her eyes worked around the living-room. Sitting on the couch was Father O'Reilly. An unwanted portion of the past. He stood and approached Anne. "Welcome home, Annie. Despite the unfortunate circumstances, it is good to see you". She looked for Terry. As if reading her thoughts he said, "She isn't here. She is at the funeral home waiting for the family. We must go now".

Fitzpatrick's Funeral Home, across the street from the Cathedral.

Quiet music playing. The candles lit. An overflowing of flowers that stifled one's breath. An Irish wake that only Mr. Fitzpatrick could orchestrate. Grief, like the rain, was everywhere.

Gradually, she approached. She was now a few feet away from the glossy, mahogany casket and took the last few steps at once. She stooped a bit and her hand lingered on the satin lining.

A tear fell.

She leaned over. She didn't want anyone to see that she was crying.

Father O'Reilly stood behind her.

"You must learn to forgive, Annie, you must learn to forgive".

As she lifted her head, she stared at the priest standing before her.

"Forgive", she replied.

"That will never come to pass".

Printed in the United States
31669LVS00005B/352-432